THE THERAVÂDA
MACHINE
AND
OTHER STORIES

ALEXX BOLLEN

OUTLET
PRESS

THE THERAVÂDA
MACHINE AND
OTHER STORIES
ISBN/SKU:9780578536354
ISBN Complete:978-0-578-53635-4
Alexx Bollen
©2019
Cover and interior art by
Melanie Piekema
Cover and interior design by
Eric J. Millar

CONTENTS

Acknowledgements:

I'd like to thank Melanie Piekema for the amazing cover art, and Eric J. Millar for his layout magic.

Special thanks to my editing helpers: Tara Sager, Erik Arneson, and Martin J. Clemens.

Thanks to John Meyers, Colin Stryker, Stephanie Quick, Craig Bollen, Roejen Razorwire of Project Archivist, and Keats Ross of We the Hallowed

And finally, extra special thanks go to the yawning maw of existential dread that made this work possible.

IN THE YEAR OF THE
GREAT PORTLAND EARTHQUAKE

It happened in the year of the Great Portland Earthquake. It wasn't an actual earthquake though. Rather, it was a seismic study done by some university or another. The study said, in essence, that the Pacific Northwest (specifically the Portland area) was due for a large earthquake. The study was based on volcanic activity; fault lines; and all sorts of other scientific esoterica. This study was picked up by the scientific media. The scientific media was then picked up by the regular media. The regular media was then picked up by everyone else. Everyone else eventually told my mother.

"Mom, it's not happening anytime soon. It's just a projection or something like that. Nothing to be concerned over."

My mother has been worrying about this since the story came out in 'respectable magazines.'

The headlines were along the lines of:

STUDY SHOWS PROJECTED DAMAGE FROM SEISMIC ACTIVITY

IN PACIFIC NW

NEW STUDY SHOWS THAT THE DORMANT PACIFIC NW VOLCANIC SUBSTRATES WILL EVENTUALLY AWAKEN

THE PACIFIC NW RIPE FOR ACCIDENT

PORTLAND ON THE EDGE OF DESTRUCTION

PORTLAND IS ALREADY DEAD

OH FUCKING CHRIST RUN! etc...

"Yes," I continued." I saw the story too."

"Well, have you thought about moving back home? There are no earthquakes in New York."

"No, I think I'll be okay out here. Besides, I don't know anyone in New York anymore. I'm too old to get a new social life."

"You know plenty of people! What about me and your father?"

"Oh come on, mom. I can't move across the country to hang out with my parents. I'm almost thirty. That's just sad."

"Well, you should come and visit then."

"Sure, soon as I get some vacation time. But, I gotta run – I think I hear some rumbling in the distance."

"That's not funny. Well, thanks for calling. Love you."

"Love you too. Tell dad I said, 'Hey'."

I lived in Portland, Oregon at the time- in an apartment building straight from the heart of the plywood and plasterboard 1970s. It was forty years into the building's existence and it showed no signs of gathering any historical value. Twenty-nine years into my existence and I was showing some wear at the edges. I was fresh out of another pointless relationship with someone I had little affection for- another one of those placeholder relationships to fill the void between birth and retirement. I was twenty-nine and burnt out on pretty much everything. The world hadn't worked out for me yet, and it certainly showed no signs of changing its direction with age.

So, I lived in this not too shitty, but certainly not that great, apartment building in Portland with a roommate I barely spoke to, and a cat that hated me. How did I know the cat hated me, you ask? Well, I had many, many reasons, foremost of which was how it looked at me. It would look at me with these cold, brutal eyes. It looked at me as if I were prey for the hunt. However, when I surreptitiously watched it looking at the couch, or the roommate, it had lovely, kind eyes... nothing like the demonic eyes it used when it looked at me, so full of bile, hate, and fury.

What made it worse was that it never scratched me. Never. Not once. If it ever hurt me physically I could have proven the cat's hatred with scars and fresh bloody scratches. But it was smarter than that. It would try to trip me when I was drunk; it would try to suffocate me when I was asleep on the couch; but its claws remained withdrawn. It refused to leave evidence of its menace.

The second major reason that I knew the cat hated me was the mouse problem. The apartment had mice. I wouldn't say infested, yet I certainly wouldn't use the singular tense. It was riddled with mice, but the traps and the cat kept back the brunt of full-infestation. Except in my room, that is. My room was trap-only. The cat would not kill mice in my room. Was the cat banned from my room you ask? No... well, yes, but the locks were terrible and that cat always found a way in. I gave up my ban eventually. But, in all the long years of nearly-infested living in a nearly-terrible apartment, the cat never lifted a paw to the mice in my room. I repeat: the thing hated me.

The last woman I dated while living there thought the cat was cute. You can't imagine how much that really bothered me. She knew all the excellent reasons for my anti-cat platform, yet she still sided with the cat. She wantonly chose my roommate's cat over my feelings. Though, I suspect she thought I was kidding about the whole thing. I only realized that after we had broken up. Not that we broke up over the cat, far from it, but it was a contributing factor. How could I love someone who was fond of my enemy? It's impossible. No one who loved that cat could be trusted to share my bed.

Now, you may be annoyed at me for telling you that I was "anti-cat" and that's fair. But I was not, nor am I anti-CATS. I was, and am, anti-CAT –singular – specifically that one stupid cat I lived with a handful of years ago. It's still alive, from what I hear; I still hate it. Every few weeks I think about stopping by my old place to visit the cat. I want to know if its feelings towards me have changed in the intervening years. I suspect it'll still stare at me maliciously while everyone else coos at how adorable it is.

Anyway, as I said, that relationship was mostly affectionless, so it wasn't that big of a deal that we broke up. After all was said and done, she was gone and I was in an apartment I didn't like with a cat who didn't like me and a closet full of dead mice in traps.

I was watching TV as a mouse ran around my floor. It was fast, and rather distracting. I could see the cat sitting on the living room couch watching it too.

My phone rang at 10pm – an unknown East Coast number. The cat got off the couch and chased the mouse under my bed. I felt the quake before it hit and listened to my father tell me that my mother was dead.

THE
MANDELA EFFECT

---

1. The Name

"I'm sure it was the BerenSTEEN Bears!"

"I know. Me too. But they're actually called the BerenSTAIN Bears. It's called the Mandela Effect."

The café was almost empty. Alicia and Amelia were talking a little too loudly. The barista was eyeballing them with every laugh and exclamation.

"Why's that?" Alicia asked.

"For Nelson Mandela. There's a bunch of people who remember him dying in the 1980s," Amelia said. "But he was actually alive until 2010 or somewhere around there... at least in this universe."

"Weird. So why do we remember the BerenstEEN universe when we live in the BerenstAIN one?"

"I dunno... well, I've heard a few sorta different ideas. I like the one that goes like this: all realities are super close to each other, and we switch through them all the time. But they're all basically the same, so we don't remember or notice when we enter a new universe, reality, or whatever. But sometimes we switch into a reality... universe... thingy that's got a significant enough difference, and we notice the difference. Like, if the reality next door was identical but the thing we call an ounce was one-trillionth of an atom lighter, there's no chance we'd notice. Or, like, if a coffee cup in a diner in Nebraska was off-white instead of true-white, some of the diner patrons would notice, but they'd most likely ignore it, or forget it the next day. But, sometimes, we slip a couple universes over and Mandela is dead in 2010 when where we left from he died in 1981. I don't know why everyone doesn't switch. It's probably just random. Anyway, that's why it's not BerenstEEN anymore... or so one theory goes."

They sat in silence for a moment. Alicia took a sip of tea.

"This is strange. Do you think it could just be a memory problem? You know, like how they say déjà vu is your brain mistiming a neuron or something like that, and it tries to catch up, so you think it happened already. Could it be something like that?" Alicia asked.

"I suppose so. I mean, I can't say that I really believe in the whole 'switching between realities in a multiverse' thing. It's just a fun idea... But, you know, it is probably because of a brain thing like you said." She paused, thinking. "Wait, now that I think of it, why would everyone's brain produce the same memory? Why would a misfiring neuron kill Nelson Mandela? He was a goddamn hero!"

"I think you've had too much coffee."

"Probably, but I just get so mad thinking about some arrogant jerk neuron killing a great man!" yelped Amelia

"You're weird," said Alecia. "I don't know why the brain would choose the same memory... that doesn't make much sense either."

"Probably chemtrails..."

"Probably."

2. *The Grass*

Luke was sitting in a park thinking about how weird it was that dead eye cells only show themselves on sunny days. He reminded himself that they're called 'floaters.' He always forgot that word.

He tried to soften his vision enough to watch the floaters move across the summer sky. Every time he focused too hard they'd dance away, elusive worms and dots across the aged film stock of his 32-year-old eyes. The other park-goers didn't pay him any attention. He wasn't sure if they were watching their own floating dead tissue.

He thought it was odd how easily the world can be changed. Some cells died, and now the world is one of translucent floating worms and amoebas. A small death many years ago turned the world into this one – his world – full of phantasmagoria, the slippery images of a life with too much attention paid.

He watched a line of white clouds follow an airplane and stood up from the green park bench. He walked across a grassy field as two teams of chubby adults played kickball. He watched a frisbee float gently into the hand of a beautiful woman around his age. No one in the park noticed the solitary man walking through their numbers. He noticed so many of them. One was wearing a shirt with a merkabah on it, a piece of what people call 'sacred geometry.' He wondered if the man wearing the shirt knew what he was wearing, or simply liked the design. He watched blades of grass wave in the spaces in his path, wondering if they ever ended up in knots. He wondered what the most tangled knot nature ever created looked like. The grass held no floaters. The grass ended at a sidewalk. The sidewalk stretched before him, right and left, north and south. He listened to the plane that was growing clouds and followed it. The park goers played kickball. The woman with the frisbee was giggling. Two blades of grass entwined for a moment. No knots were made.

3. The Game

Years ago in a coffee shop, a man and a woman played a board game. They had just met. It was time well spent. The coffee shop was closing and the woman went to the restroom. The man got nervous waiting since the place was already well cleaned and the barista obviously wanted to shut down. He got too antsy and left, waiting outside. He didn't see her again.   His walk home was lonely and full of doubt.

She chatted with the barista, wondering when her new friend would get out of the bathroom. He never did. She looked for him outside and found nothing. She walked home wondering what had gone wrong.

Years ago a street light was flickering. It made the plants on the corner look like they were filmed in slow motion. A young woman avoided that corner out of habit. She disliked the strobe effect. One evening, many years ago, she would have seen a twenty-dollar bill laying crumpled next to the sidewalk. She would have picked it up.

She would have walked to the store and bought a bottle of wine. She would have been shot on the way home by a stray bullet from a domestic dispute three blocks over. She would have watched the pavement as her blood mixed with the shitty white wine flowing from jagged glass.

But the streetlight was broken, so the wine stayed pure.

4. *The Mirror*

Amelia wrote her name on her left arm in permanent marker.

She stared into a mirror at midnight, a single candle the only light.

She imagined, focused, strained at her reflection.

She tried to switch places with her reflection. To be the person with her name written on her right arm.

The burnt image flame echoed in her closed eyes as she tried to sleep. The room smelled of wax.

In the morning she woke and looked at her arms. Her name was written on both.

She had no idea if it worked, or if she had put herself into such a hypnotic state that she repeated the letters on her other arm. She wondered how she could have managed such perfect script with her non-dominant hand. She wondered if it worked. Could she now be in the universe next door? Did her intention to shift reality become reality. She thought about the universe she had tried to reach. How could she test it? Could she ask Alicia? She thought of ways to prove something unprovable, but her sheets were warm and soon she was asleep again.

The universes paid no attention.

Later that day Alicia and Amelia were sitting together in a small living room. It was sparsely furnished, but elegant in its way. The walls were that perfect shade of white that only people well-versed in decoration could identify and prefer.

"Oh, by the way, how do you pronounce the children's book about the bears?" Amelia said.

"Haven't we discussed this before? The whole Mandela effect thing? I swore that we did."

"Yeah, I know, just, you know, go along with it. I'm trying to see if something I tried last night worked."

"Umm, okay. Well, it's the BerenSTAIN Bears. But some people think that it was BerenSTEEN Bears. Why do you ask?"

"And you knew it as BerenSTEEN like me. That's why it's a thing... like those people who thought Mandela died years ago."

"Yeah, in the late 80s, but I never thought that. That's just part of the theory. When I was a kid it was BerenSTAIN just like the books say."

"But, last time you said you remembered it like I did. BerenSTEEN."

"Nope. I've always thought it was STAIN. That's why I found it weird that all those people, you too I guess, thought it was STEEN."

"But... wait... I could have sworn that you were one of the STEENS. Wasn't that, like, the whole point of the conversation?"

"Sorry Amelia. I'm a STAIN girl, always was, always will be. I sent you that link to the story, you probably just thought I was agreeing with them."

"Shit... yeah... I guess that could be it. I could have sworn... eh, it doesn't matter in the end."

"Not really. It is just a children's book. To be honest I can't remember a single plot from them, just vaguely recall having them read to me."

"Me too. Strange how that works."

5. The Hill

A few years ago a Buddha-like character established himself on a mountain near town. He preached pretty phrases and attracted pretty people. The locals got nervous. He remained calm. Groups of like-minded people walked up the mountain to see him. He took a bit of money – only enough to live. He let people give him gifts – only small things to show affection. He tried.

In those years the locals drew attention to the buddha on the hill. The police were involved. He was arrested for dodging his taxes. His followers were livid but did nothing dramatic. They eventually dispersed into the valley and forgot his words. He was let free after a year then disappeared into a crowd downtown.

If, and only if, one nervous man did not call his nervous neighbor, things would have changed. If he had remained silent, the world would have eventually had another sacred book. But, as it often happens, things went the wrong way, and those people were left in want.

6. The Puddle

Once again, Luke sat in the park by his apartment. He watched the puddle between his feet. The reflection of the sky made the world brown, twilight. He watched the puddle sky ripple in the small breeze. He felt his eyes throb. His face grew hot. He looked at the puddle-sky world and it turned to blue. His eyes throbbed. His face reddened.

"They just don't match, and the matches are wet from the rain."

Where did he know that line from? Did he even have matches? He was sure he didn't, but maybe in his backpack a bit of out-of-time flotsam had appeared to light a cigarette which he hadn't had in nearly five years.

He leaned back and felt the harsh bench hit his back. The sky was a blue mess of floating blobs and erratic clouds. He watched planes move as parallel clouds followed in their wake. He waited for his breath to catch, his face to cool. He looked back at the puddle world, now a glowing, vibrant, blue. The plane clouds were long gone. He looked at the park and found it empty. He wondered what happened to the couple on the blanket, the kid by the basketball court. He stepped in the puddle universe and watched it subsumed by scattering waves. The grass near his foot billowed, entwining two blades for a moment. The air smelled of chrysanthemum as he walked he passed what he knew was a rose garden. He was sure it was a rose garden. He needed confirmation. The street heading north was closed for construction. He chose to go to the bookstore a bit further east. It was a thirty-minute walk, but he needed to know.

The bookstore wasn't busy. He was thankful for this. The woman at the front desk pointed him to the back corner of the store.

The children's section was thankfully free of children. He didn't want to look like a weirdo studying kids' books by himself.

He chanted in a low whisper.

"Beren-stain… Beren-stEEN… Beren-stain…"

He read the cover a dozen times.

Berenstain.

He was no longer home.

He was in the puddle.

A woman stood next to him staring at the book in his hand. He looked into her eyes. She looked into his.

"You too?" She asked.

He nodded and held out the book with a shaking hand.

Above the store, the sky was clear of parallel clouds.

A
PERVASIVE THOUGHT

A cold, wet, drop from a drain pipe hits the back of my neck. I'm awake already. That was excessive. The universe is kind of a shithead. I think it's because I have a leather jacket and I don't eat meat. That's kind of hypocritical, right? Hell if I know. I have little sense of what is right and wrong in the world. All I know is that a non-potable line of distraction just slipped down my spine and I'm walking with no sort of destination.

I wish I smoked cigarettes. I feel like it would be a nice sort of slum-romance to drag on a cigarette in the rain, all mysterious and cool. But I'm healthy, and it's not that rainy out. I'm a healthy hypocrite with poor timing in regards to passing under leaky drains. Not even a cool leather jacket and an unhealthy disregard for my lungs could make up for a shiver of rain running down my back on a relatively dry evening. Maybe I should get a walking stick, or a cane. That wouldn't help either. There's no escaping the self, no matter how far you walk in any given direction, no matter what decorations you wear.

It's been eleven years since she died. I should be over it already. But I keep picturing her rotting under all that dirt. I imagine the inside of her casket... her coffin... whatever it's called. I keep picturing its stupid white silk interior with my stupid dead friend rotting her stupid dead flesh away on top of it. Every time I think about it I lose like four days of productive alone time. She invites herself into the slow calm places between thoughts of everyday life. It always starts with her stupid dead face. It wasn't stupid in life. I should probably mention that. She had a very nice face in life. But now it's a smelly rotten mess in that dumb casket... coffin... box... thing.

Or maybe it's done being actively terrible now. Maybe all the awful part of rotting is over and now she's desiccated, a pile of bones and cloth, like a cast-off cicada shell crackling under foot. I fucking hate that. I fucking hate that she could be finished.

I even tried to visit her grave once. It's in that cemetery by the highway that goes to the suburbs. I don't remember the name of the cemetery. I suppose it doesn't matter. I turned around half way there. I wouldn't have recognized her in the grass that grew around her headstone. I suppose I shouldn't have expected to, but that grass is all that's left of her now and it probably looks like the same green nonsense that kids play soccer on, and dads mow on the weekend. It's just faceless, pointless, grass wasting water and covering up my dead friend. So I never actually visited, but I did picture it pretty often.

I think it's maybe 7pm. I have no idea. I lost my phone weeks ago and hate watches. I know, I know: phones are important. But I don't have many friends to call, and my family isn't around much. I don't mind not knowing what time it is, but I miss playing Scrabble on my phone. Scrabble is fun. In fact my dead friend and I played Scrabble together often. She wasn't dead back then though. This was during the days when Scrabble could only be played on a physical board. I had a great one that spun around on some kind of mechanism so everyone could see the tiles as upright when it was their turn. She wasn't great at Scrabble. I used to play shittier words so she would feel like she had a chance. One time she won because of this. I was tanking my game so she would be close in points. Then, like a shot out of nowhere towards endgame, she hits a bingo on a triple word. It was like 80 points. All I had in my rack were vowels, an R, and an N. I tried to figure something out. I lost by like 10 points. She was super happy. I never told her that I didn't play full-strength. Now that she's all rotten and underground, I don't think she minds that I didn't try as hard as I could.

Yeah, it must be like 7pm. It's got that feel to it. The sky is getting dirty yellow. I keep thinking I should get a drink. I like to have a few before bed. I can't sleep that well normally, especially when she's floating around my memories. I keep picturing that one time when we were more than friends. When, and I'm sorry to be so blunt, I keep picturing getting a blow job from her. Horrible, right? But there she is in full technicolor with my dick in her mouth. Her mouth is gone now. It's dried out, held together with mortician's twine. I think they wire your jaw shut when you get prepared for burial. I'm not sure about that. But I keep thinking about that blowjob.

It's such a stupid thing to get upset about remembering. We were young and drunk. I remember how it felt to kiss her. But that doesn't bother me as much for some reason.

Some nights it's all I can do to not vomit. I wish I could stop picturing that – my manhood in her dead face. It's close to 8pm and my stomach hurts from thinking about her. I wish more water would hit my neck so I could shut my stupid brain off. There's a bar like five blocks from here that doesn't seem to mind me sitting there and reading a book. I guess I should walk over there and drink a bit. I like to have a few drinks so I can turn my head off before bed and stop picturing awful things.

According to the clock above the bar it's 12:23am. My stomach feels better. I'm warm from booze. The bartender is nice to me. I haven't thought about my dead friend in a few minutes, except that I just did. I hope I can sleep tonight without imagining myself in her. It's a really distracting thought. I wonder if this will ever go away? I guess I'll find out.

The guy sitting next to me, who I sorta know, is talking to me. We have a chat. I don't remember anything he says, not from the alcohol, but from the boredom. I think he was talking about sports, or maybe it was something to do with a video he was watching. I think it was a video- probably about cats. They always want to talk about cats.

He's talking about stuff he did in college now. He's pretty drunk. I think his story is funny. Well, I don't know if it's actually funny, but I do laugh when I think I'm supposed to. He looks happy. I'm pretty good at timing my fake laughs and "yeahs" when I'm not paying full attention. I wish I could start reading again without my bar friend finding it offensive. I have my book under my whiskey coaster at the moment. I like reading at bars. I know some people think that it's anti-social, but the white-noise of humans interacting is comforting and distracts me from my own thoughts. I think I'm getting drunk tonight. I hope I can sleep.

The walk home is fraught with low hanging branches. I'm like one of those mad, inflatable things in front of car-lots as I try to bend in half to avoid the obstacles. This comes with a fair amount of swerving. A cop car rolls by slowly and shines a light in my face. I put my hand up to shield my eyes and say hello. They seem happy with this answer and drive off. I guess they were looking for a different inflatable man. I never know how to feel when this sort of thing happens. I'm a white guy. I guess you should know that. If I were a different color I'm sure that situation would have a different outcome. That's unfair. But, I mean, should I feel grateful? I did just get blinded by a cop and didn't have to show ID or have to get shot. That's pretty nice. Or should I be upset because not everyone gets this treatment? I'm too drunk to think about this stuff. My eyeballs hurt and there's a cop-light shaped object floating in my vision.

I wake up on the couch. The way the light is blinding me makes me think it's before noon. My neck is making terrible noises. It feels like I got some loose dirt in it last night. Everything is crunchy. In the bathroom I can't look down to pee and wet my sock a bit. Who cares? I have more socks. I take two aspirin with a glass of water, my neck breaking with the effort of swallowing. I go to my actual bed. It's really cold. I fall back asleep. I dream of soft skin. I'm erect when I wake up. My neck feels a bit better. I feel the blanket pushing back on my penis. I think of the time my dead friend gave me a blowjob. I wish I didn't think of it so often. I guess I don't think about her that often, really. It happens in waves. It may be years at a time when she's just a faint memory. Then, out of the clear blue sky, I remember that night. Once I remember that, I have days of ruinous thoughts to look forward to.

Have I tried masturbating to the memory, you ask? Of course I have. I thought it could cure me. Like that old thing about the hair of the dog that bit you. Have you ever tried getting off while thinking about a rotting girl? It's not fun, or helpful. So, yeah, no more of that. I lay in bed and wish I could do something about it. I decide to write a letter.

Elle,

I'm really sorry that I never visited your grave. I couldn't face it after the wake. And by the time I felt strong enough I couldn't find it and didn't know anyone who knew where you were buried. I feel shitty about that. Not nearly as shitty as I feel about how I keep remembering you. I hope that you can't, I don't know, sense my thoughts from wherever it is that you are, assuming you are anywhere. I hope you are somewhere and that wherever you are you can't know my thoughts. I don't mean it. It's just that I tend towards catastrophic thinking and that goes double with you since the worst thing ever happened. Anyway, it's day two of my brain torturing myself with memories and I thought, hey, why not address the issue. Yeah. So I keep thinking about that thing we did the one time. You know what I mean. Look, I know it's stupid. But, as I said, I tend towards catastrophic thinking. I'm really sorry. I remember all this other great stuff about you as well. Of course those memories don't haunt me nearly as often because I am aging and my brain is rebelling against itself. I'm almost glad you didn't have to go through this aging shit. You get to be forever young and beautiful and hardly marred by the world. You're eternal in your death.

That's kind of nice. Anyway, I'm fat now and I keep thinking about us when I was young and thin and we did that thing and I'm super sorry that I keep thinking about that. But, you should know that I think about the other, less stupid things, too. After all these years I think that's pretty good testament to your influence on the rest of us aging idiots. Okay, well, I hope you're somewhere and you're content there. Maybe we'll see each other again and then you can slap my fat, dead face because I'm a terrible friend that keeps thinking about something so trivial that meant almost nothing to us while we were both alive and breathing. I'm sure you'd forgive me- you were always good like that. I wish you were still here.

Yours,
######

  I put the letter in a drawer on top of the others I've written over the years. This time it took two more days to stop thinking about her.

THE
THERAVÂDA MACHINE

I first woke to the sounds of electricity on a random Tuesday morning. The air smelled of smoke. A pulsing blue light seeped in from under the door. I dressed myself, for I slept in a pair of boxer shorts and nothing else. Once sufficiently clothed as to avoid embarrassment, I left the room.

My bedroom opened to the living area of the apartment. It was lit with that same blue light, though stronger, steadier. Wisps of delicate smoke wafted in from the kitchen. I entered the bathroom and switched on the horribly bright light. The bathroom smelled of burning plastic as I splashed water on my face. I brushed my teeth and hair. I felt much better.

I left the bathroom feeling refreshed. The living room was still blue; the trails of smoke still carried on their subtle currents. I walked through the room leaving a misty-blue wake in the smoke.

The kitchen window let in too much sun. My eyes always hurt

in the morning. I walked around the three men and opened the fridge. I felt very silly when I realized that I had orange juice. Why did I feel the need to brush my teeth? Damn my memory. I filled a glass from the filtered carafe instead. I sat at the kitchen table and sipped heavily from the crisp, cold water.

"Ahhhh," I said to myself, "cold water in the morning is nearly as good as orange juice."

I finished the first glass so quickly that I stood to get another. The fridge door hit the back of one of the men sitting on my kitchen floor. I apologized and sat back down to drink another glass of crisp, delicious, filtered water.

There were three men on my kitchen floor. They sat cross-legged on a blue blanket made of a strange, unfamiliar material. Between them was an expanse of wires, circuit boards, soldering irons, and two wooden boxes full to brimming with technological ephemera.

The men wore gray mechanic's overalls. They seemed content in their work.

I thought to ask them what they were doing, but I felt rude interrupting.

I left the apartment to drive to work in my sputtering car. It left a cloud of blue, oil-rich, smoke in its wake. I wondered if I could fix it. I wondered if the men in my kitchen could fix it.

My work was done in a nondescript office situated in the center of a complex of other similar offices. It was a good job. They paid me on the 1st and 15th of every month. The money they paid me with was enough to keep my lovely apartment and functional car. The work I did was very detail oriented and important. It was important, but hard to describe to someone outside of the company. I filled out many forms. I counted many boxes of things. I made sure the people in the next row took lunch breaks and arrived on time.

I was, at the time, middle management. That, at the time, meant I could become upper management eventually. My boss was upper management. I liked my boss. He sometimes got us breakfast pastries on Fridays when the spirit was upon him. Once, during a particularly festive winter party, he provided us with alcoholic drinks and gave us envelopes full of extra pay. It was a good place to work. The only part I didn't enjoy was wearing a tie. I've always felt slightly strangled by ties. The thought of ties makes me itch. But clothes make the man, my very nice boss said. I agreed with my boss often. Though I was unsure about his belief in the wearing of ties.

I went straight to my girlfriend's apartment after work. She was hosting a gathering of family members and I was to be displayed for them. The night went well. The mood was convivial. Her family seemed to like me. I thought her mother was especially charming. She smiled in exactly the same way as my girlfriend. It was easy.

———————————————

It was a numberless Thursday night; I was spending the evening with my girlfriend. She was a wonderful girlfriend. We went out every Thursday, Saturday, and Sunday night. Sometimes we went out on other nights as well, but those weren't set in stone. We liked seeing each other at least three times a week. We left the restaurant and, after a short conversation, decided to go to my apartment. Her apartment was also very nice, but we liked to switch back and forth to avoid overusing one or the other. It was her idea. It was a great idea. Her car was better than mine, so she drove us there.

We walked the short distance from the parking lot to the stairs leading to my apartment. My apartment sat above a defunct café. The café had been shut down for over a year. The tables, chairs, and coffee equipment sat exactly where they were the day the doors were locked for the last time. I looked through the window to watch the dust accumulate every time I went home. The steps leading to my apartment were made of wood and had begun to sag. I didn't know who the landlord was anymore, so I fixed them as they sank too far. The landlord also ran the café, back when it still was a café. When he shut it down, he also stopped cashing my rent checks. It was six months before I stopped writing them. I kept every penny I owed him though, in case I was discovered and the money demanded. I am no apartment thief. I was, however, not so keen to find out who I was beholden to. I really liked my apartment and was afraid to lose it.

We entered my apartment on that Thursday night after navigating the sagging steps. The blue smoke was heavier than it had been that morning. The three men on my kitchen floor worked diligently. I took a bottle of wine and two glasses from the cupboard. We sat in the living room and I poured us some wine. It was red. She always picked out the bottles for us. I don't know much about wine.

"There are three men in your kitchen," she said.

"Oh, yes. I don't think they drink. But I can offer them the other bottle if you're uncomfortable drinking alone," I said.

"No, that's okay. What are they doing in your kitchen?"

"They are constructing some sort of electronic device. They've been at it since Tuesday morning, at least."

"Oh," she said.

"I don't know how long it will take. It seems pretty complicated."

"Yes, it does seem like pretty intricate work. Who are they?" she asked.

"I'm not sure. They have uniforms on. I assume they are professionals," I explained.

"You haven't asked them?"

"No, they seemed too busy."

"True."

"Want to watch a movie or play some cards before bed?" I asked.

"I think a movie would be fine. Can we finish the one from Sunday? I liked it before we distracted each other," she said, giggling.

"We can try," I said, touching her hand with mine.

———————————

A few weeks later I woke up on an unremarkable Tuesday morning. My bedroom smelled heavily of ozone. I got out of bed and dressed to the pulsing blue light from under my door. After the bathroom rituals of morning I went to the kitchen. I filled my glass from the carafe of filtered water. The air smelled metallic, with the faintest hint of burnt plastic. It was rather nice in its way. It smelled something like the air after a spring rain on asphalt. I tried to remember the word for the smell. I couldn't remember the word. I enjoyed the smell and drank my water.

The three men were sitting on their blue blanket fiddling at wires and plastic pieces. I thought that they had rotated one seat over at some point recently. It was hard to tell because they all wore gray coveralls and had very similar faces. I thought the thing which they were building, having no idea what it was actually meant to look like, looked great. So I told them so.

"That looks great," I said.

The three men sitting on my kitchen floor looked up at me in my kitchen chair. Their faces showed no emotion, but I felt that I had broken our implied agreement that we would remain quiet to one another.

"Sorry," I mumbled.

They turned in unison back to their work. I felt bad that I had interrupted. My drive to work was guilt-ridden.

The rest of the day at work was rough. I kept thinking about how I ruined their morning. I wondered if I should get them a gift to make up for it, a fresh bundle of wires or some electrical tape. My coworkers failed to notice my distraction. I was very efficient at my work. I would not be put off by a little distracted thinking.

On my way home, I stopped by a store that sold electronics. The clerk was very friendly. He recommended that I buy a boxed set of tools and wires. I thought it was a perfect gift for an apology.

I drove home from the store wondering if I should wrap the gift. As I looked through the window into the dusty café I decided to keep it unwrapped, casual.

I opened the door to my apartment and smelled the burning rubber ozone of my kitchen. The three men on my kitchen floor were still working, undaunted by my arrival or earlier interruption. I opened a bottle of beer with the handle of the kitchen drawer and sat down. I opened the boxed set of wires and tools and carefully placed it between man number one and man number three. Man number two was considering a small spot on the device very carefully. He looked up, thinking. He caught my eye line, and I swear that he raised his lips in the slightest hint of a smile. I took that as a sign that I had done well. Our fractured relationship was healed.

I drank my beer and watched them build. The windows grew dark. The blue light of their work kept the tools visible. I wondered if I should turn on a light. I dared not risk asking them. I opened another beer and moved to the couch. I watched a movie and sipped idly at the slowly warming bottle. It was a comfortable night at home. Just me, some beers, and the three men in my kitchen quietly building their machine.

Some weeks later my girlfriend and I were sitting on my couch play fighting each other's fingers. It was a nice, cool evening. The windows were open and the burning rubber smell was barely noticeable.

"How are they doing?" she asked.

"Who?"

"The men in the kitchen."

"Oh, about the same I think. It's hard to tell. The machine makes a nice humming noise now."

"That's good. I wonder what it does. Have they ever said anything?" she asked quietly, so as to not distract the three men on my kitchen floor.

"No, they haven't said a word. One did smile at me once, I

think."

"Oh?"

"Yes, I gave them an apology gift. He noticed and smirked," I explained.

"That's nice. What did you have to apologize for?"

"I interrupted them that morning. I said 'it was looking good' or something like that. They looked very angry at being interrupted. So I picked up a nice kit of wires and clippers and such from that electronics place in town."

"What a thoughtful gift. They seem happy," she said with a smile on her lips.

"They do seem happy. Shall we go to bed now?" I asked.

"That would make me very happy."

I brushed a hair from her forehead then led her by the hand to my bedroom. It was lovely and cool inside. The blue light seeping from under the door lit our love and eventual sleep. It was a lovely evening.

The morning was bright. I had left the curtain open enough to shock early eyes. My girlfriend was not in bed. I was saddened by this. One of the things I enjoyed in life was the look of her face full of pillow lines. I walked to the bathroom. Everything smelled of burning rubber, with a hint of something new. It was a familiar smell that I couldn't place. The bathroom was uneventful except for some blood in my toothpaste spit. I worried about that. I took care of my teeth and gums.

The kitchen hummed. The machine was causing the floor to vibrate. It was pleasant on my bare feet. I filled a glass from my filtered carafe and sat down. The three men and one woman sat in the corners of a blue blanket. The woman, my girlfriend, had a tube running from her arm into the machine. She seemed to be okay with this. I was concerned though.

"What are you doing down there?" I asked.

The three men and one woman looked to me in unison. The men seemed irritated.

"I was just trying to talk to her," I said to the three men. "Sorry to interrupt."

The three men looked back at the machine.

"I wanted some water. They signaled me to sit down. I felt rude refusing. The floor tickles."

She smiled broadly at me.

"Oh, well that's okay then. Do you know what it is?"

"I don't. But it seems to need some blood to work. They haven't taken much at all."

"That's also good. I'd hate for you to lose too much blood. I like you."

"That's very nice to hear. I like you too. We should have dinner tonight," she said.

"That sounds nice. Do you think you'll be much longer with them?" I asked, gesturing with my head to the three men on my kitchen floor.

"I'm not sure. But I get the impression that we're not going to be long at all. How about you call me on your lunch break? We can make plans."

She was smiling and happy. Her tube had a very small, very slow, stream of blood moving within it.

"Sure, that's great. Well, I'm going to get ready," I said.

I got prepared for work. I kissed her cheek before I left, making sure to not disrupt the other three on the blanket. Work was busy and seemed to move quickly. I called my girlfriend at lunch and made plans to meet her at my apartment later. It felt like a long time from lunch to leaving. I was excited to have dinner with her. I thought about places to eat as I finished my work.

My apartment was glowing a bright, radiant, blue as I entered. The floor felt like a joy buzzer. The machine was blurry from its oscillation. The three men and one woman sat at their corners. I opened the refrigerator and got a beer. I opened the beer and sat down at the kitchen table. My girlfriend smiled at me. The three men stayed immobile.

"Hi!" she said excitedly, "I'm starved. Shall we get ready to go to dinner?"

"I'd like that. I am going to change clothes. Would you care to join me?"

"That sounds fun! Aren't you glad you gave me a drawer of my very own?"

"I am glad. Should you unplug now?"

"Oh, yes, I forgot about this," she said, raising her arm with the tube hanging from it. "Gentleman, I am going to remove this tube."

They turned their heads in unison to her. They looked very angry.

She pulled the tube out of her arm. Man number two grabbed her hand.

"Hey!" she said.

I grabbed the man's arm and pulled. His arm broke off at the shoulder. The fingers on his arm lost their strength and his grip failed. The detached arm dropped to the blue blanket.

"Oh no!" I yelped in an embarrassingly high voice. "Sorry! I didn't mean to do that!"

"Are you okay?" my girlfriend asked the man with one arm. She sounded deeply concerned for him.

The two men with two arms looked at the machine. The man with one arm looked impotently at his arm now lying in his lap.

"I think that's normal," I said. "They would be concerned if it wasn't. How about we go to the bedroom and dress?"

"Perfect idea! Pardon me gentlemen on the blanket. I hope his lack of arm doesn't trouble you too much."

They sat unperturbed.

We went to my bedroom and stripped to nothing. We made love on my bed which was vibrating from the machine in the kitchen. It was lovely.

We dressed and went to a Mexican restaurant we both enjoyed. It was a nice dinner. Her arm showed no sign of distress. I didn't feel particularly bad about the man's arm. He must know that I wouldn't have done it if I knew the damage that it would cause. We walked home to my apartment, arm in arm. It was a very nice night.

———————————————

It was almost three months to the day from the arrival of the men and their machine when I asked her to move into my apartment. I had realized that we spent a lot of time together and it seemed silly to keep traveling to do so. We discussed whether we should ask the three men in the kitchen if they cared if she moved in. We decided that since they didn't pay rent (not that I did, but the apartment was in my name) they shouldn't have a vote in who lived there.

We had some trouble moving in the larger items since the three men in the kitchen partially blocked entry to the living area. But, in the end, we managed. She and I shared an apartment and it was perfect. She even commented that the subtle hum of the machine helped her make love. She was very brave with what she shared with me.

The three men on a blue blanket kept at their work. The man with one arm worked slower, but with no less dull professionalism. By that point the machine looked like a tiny city. Antennas and spires rose out from its body like skyscrapers above clouds. The blue light and the lovely hum increased in intensity as the days and weeks pressed on. The arm that was removed was wrapped around the base of the machine. It seemed to be melting into it, day by day. I wondered if I should offer them some of my blood. I thought that I should wait until they brought it up. The three men on the blue blanket on my kitchen floor didn't appear to like casual chat.

The night my girlfriend moved in we got too drunk. We stumbled into the kitchen for more drinks and fell on one of the three men sitting on my kitchen floor. It was one of the men who still had two arms. The man crumbled into a pile of clothes and swirling dust. We, my girlfriend and I, couldn't help but giggle. The machine was unharmed. We coughed up his dust and stumbled back to the couch. It was a good night.

The morning after we got too drunk and broke one of the three men sitting on my kitchen floor was a difficult one. I awoke on the couch with my girlfriend curled up next to me. Her head was resting on my lap. She looked sweet lying there. I didn't want to wake her, but my neck felt like gravel. The room was spinning slightly. I needed to move. So I slipped out from under her, placing her head gently on a handy pillow. The room was not the same blue. It did not smell like burning rubber. I didn't notice the change until I had brushed my teeth and thrown water on my face. My girlfriend was still asleep when I exited the bathroom. That's when I noticed that there was no blue light, no smell of burning rubber. I walked to my kitchen. Two men (one with only one arm) and a pile of clothes were sat on a blue blanket. The machine was humming. There was no blue light. The men stared at the machine, unmoving.

I got my water from the filtered carafe and sat at the kitchen table. I thought that I would watch them for a little while before waking up my girlfriend. She looked very comfortable lying on the couch. The two men and their three arms looked at me. Their faces had grown sallow since they had arrived. They looked older. The machine looked great. You could barely see the arm at its base. They stared at me like I was a part of their machine. I smiled and nodded. I felt that would be safe since they weren't actually working at the moment. They did not respond. My neck felt horrible. I got some aspirin from the cabinet where we keep bottles of things like aspirin and multivitamins. I swallowed two white pills with some filtered water. It was cold and delicious.

My girlfriend said, "good morning."

She had awakened while I was getting aspirin.

"Would you like some aspirin or water?" I asked.

"Some water would be lovely. I see that the blue light is off."

"Yes," I said as I got her a glass of water from the filtered carafe, "I hope it wasn't because of us."

"Hmmm. Should we try and ask? It looks like they aren't working right now. Maybe they won't mind?"

"I don't know," I said, looking intently at the man directly across from the table. His eyes looked like they were unfocused, blank. "This isn't their normal behavior. What do you think?"

My girlfriend sat next to me. She placed her chin on her fist. She looked like she was really thinking about the situation.

"Well, I think that we should ask them if they need help," she said, determined. "They are down a man and an arm. It seems only polite to offer some help."

"That seems like a good idea. You know, you're pretty great," I said, grinning stupidly.

"You're pretty great too," she said with an even broader smile.

"Who should ask? Did they talk when they asked for your blood?"

"No, they were silent. They motioned for me to sit down. When they got the implements out it sort of seemed obvious what they wanted."

"Dang, they've never spoken to me either. I guess I'll ask unless you want to."

"I don't mind either way," she said.

"Okay, well I'll go ahead and ask. I was alone here when they arrived. I suppose it's my responsibility."

The two men and one pile of clothes were sat in their normal spots. They made up an unmoving triangle of plain, uniformed people.

"Excuse me, men on my kitchen floor," I said.

The two men with viable, non-dusted heads, turned towards me and my girlfriend, impassive.

"Well... we... my girlfriend and I..." I said, motioning to her, "wanted to know if work on the machine on the floor was stalled because of our drunken tumble last night."

The two men and the pile kept staring at me and my girlfriend. They did not seem angry this time.

"Umm... well, we feel somewhat bad about knocking into your friend... colleague... other guy. We thought that maybe the machine... we call the thing you're building 'the machine' – that maybe you stopped working on it because of us. Is there anything we can do to make it up to you?"

The two men who still had recognizable bodies looked at each other. They made no sound, but it looked as if they were communicating. After a few seconds they turned back to me and my girlfriend. Their eyes were once again a clear, intelligent, blue.

"Welcome," They said in unison. Their voices were deep, strong. Their voices had the same resonance as the humming of the machine. "Welcome but unneeded."

They shifted back to staring blankly at the machine. Their eyes slowly clouding.

"Great!" my girlfriend exclaimed, "I'm so glad that they are still okay. I feel a ton lighter!"

"Me too," I said. "They'll get back to it very soon I'm sure."

We sat in silence for a few minutes. The apartment was very quiet. The single light bulb in the kitchen cast everything a dirty yellow.

"I miss the hum," she said.

"Me too. I miss the blue light," I said.

"Me too," she said.

I was eating lunch at the kitchen table. I had made egg salad and was eating it between slices of toasted rye bread. The toasted rye chaffed the corners of my mouth a bit. I wished that I hadn't toasted it. But, I thought, who am I to complain? The men on the floor are dealing with far worse than a dry toast injury. I ate my sandwich silently while watching the machine, the two men, and one dust pile. I finished my sandwich and licked the corner of my mouth. I hated that feeling. I looked at the machine and wondered if I should do something. I wished that I knew more about machines and engineering; then I could be useful. I hated feeling so useless in my own space.

"Excuse me, men on the kitchen floor," I said, "I'm sorry to belabor the point but maybe you'd like some help today? I can't help but notice that progress seems to have stalled."

They sat without any sign that they had heard me. The machine was as quiet as ever. The machine seemed ominous in just how much nothing it was doing. The machine seemed to be feeding off the ambient nothing, concentrating it into a super-nothing, daring itself to move a molecule.

I watched the nothing machine. I saw it do nothing. Please understand me when I say that it DID nothing. It sat there like a verb. It radiated nothing. It imbued the room with nothing. It sat without noise or movement.

I shuddered.

"Well, I guess if you need me you know where to find me. Can I least offer you some food or refreshment? I won't be offended if you say no."

They sat on the blue carpet. A mote of dust feathered itself down onto the machine. The leader, I called the one nearest the wall 'the leader,' finally turned his head to me. The dust mote must have acted as some kind of switch.

"You may sit," his voice sounded like the creaking of old floorboards, like rusted hinges forced into action.

"Oh, thank you. Where?"

With the barest tilt of his head he indicated the dust pile that was once his third.

"Oh, should I move him first? Or, just, you know, sit in him?"

The man on the blanket, the leader, simply moved his head again, indicating the pile of clothes and dust.

I felt awkward sitting in his friend. But I was never much of an engineer, so I left it to the expert. I sat down, crossed legged, on top of the pile that was once the third man sitting on the blue blanket in my kitchen. I looked into the leader's dull blue eyes and waited. Nothing happened. And not the all-encompassing, disturbing Nothing of the machine, but the simple, normal, everyday nothing of sitting on a blanket with some of the fellas. I looked at the one-armed man. He offered no more information than the leader. I wondered if I should do something. I sat there for what seemed like an hour before my girlfriend came unexpectedly into the kitchen. She wasn't due home till dinner.

"Arhsh gmmm jeeks," she said.

"What? I'm sorry but I can't hear you properly. Shouldn't you be at school?"

"Ahhhmmmmphhh huhhhhh ffffff shhhhhh," she said. "Kuuu faaaaaa shhhhh?"

"I'm sorry. I can't hear you. Let me stand up," I said, standing.

The arm of the leader shot out at a blazing speed to stop me. I panicked and drew my arm away while falling into the wall. He missed his attempted grab.

My head put a head-shaped dent in the drywall.

"Oh my! Are you okay?" my girlfriend exclaimed.

"I'm okay. I broke the wall with my head though. That's unfortunate," I said.

"It's fine. We can fix it," she said calmly. "Why didn't you answer me? I was screaming for nearly an hour!"

"What? You just got here," I said.

"No, I have been yelling and trying to pull you up from the floor but there was something stopping my arm. I was concerned!" she said.

At that moment I realized just how much I loved her. She was a very sweet person.

"Oh, I'm so sorry," I said. "I was trying to help the men on the blue carpet in my kitchen. Why are you home so early?"

"Early? I'm right on time."

"Really? I just had lunch. What time is it?"

"It's just about six," she said, sounding worried.

"Really? I didn't notice how long I was there. Did that happen when you visited them?"

"No, time worked perfectly back then," she said.

"It's just as well. I didn't have much to do today anyway. What would you like for dinner?"

"I guess we could go to the Indian place with the good naan," she said.

"That would be lovely," I said. "Let me wash up and get some clean clothes. These are covered in dust."

"Okay. I'll watch some TV while you're at it."

"Good. If the men on the blue carpet in the kitchen ask why I left please tell them that I wanted to have dinner with you."

"Okay! Wash well!" She said and kissed my cheek.

I went to the bedroom to change. The machine did nothing. Even the earlier, ominous Nothing was long gone.

My girlfriend was a waitress at the time. She was studying, when not waitressing or being with me, to be a psychiatrist. It was hard at times to balance everything, but she was a very talented and dedicated person.

I still went to work every day. The people in my office never noticed a thing. I left thoughts of the men and their machine at home, for the most part. They were our secret, my girlfriend's and mine.

The men on my kitchen had stopped working. They showed no emotion on their faces, but we thought they looked sad. The blue blanket was collecting a film of dust. Day by day the city-like machine looked colder and colder. The apartment worked in two ways: The life of my girlfriend and I; and the life of the two men and one pile of dusty clothes on the kitchen floor. It was a delicate balance. We balanced it well.

It was forty-nine days after I had sat with the men on the kitchen floor. My girlfriend was jittery. Her morning routine had changed. She did not sit in the kitchen. She did not change from her sleeping clothes. I sat in bed and listened to her pace.

She entered our bedroom after thirty minutes of pacing holding a thermometer.

"Are you sick?" I asked.

"No," she responded, "I'm not sick. I'm pregnant with your child."

"Really? That's fantastic!" I said, standing to embrace her.

We hugged and she made noises of contentment. I felt the wet tip of the thermometer on my back. I realized it was a pregnancy test.

"You're happy about this?" she asked.

"I can't think of anything that would make me happier!" I said.

"That's very good to hear. I was worried."

"Nothing to be worried about. I'm incredibly happy to be the other half of this. I think we will make very good parents."

"Yes. I think we will."

We held each other silently for a long time.

We both took the day off.

It was one of the best moments of my life.

It was a few days after she told me of our coming baby that we decided to try and talk to the men in my kitchen again.

We put it off for weeks.

My girlfriend and I were doing very, very well. She loved me. I loved her. We waited anxiously through our work days to see each other at night. The apartment was darker in those days. The hum hadn't returned. But we were perfect and happy.

The two men sat on the blue blanket. The pile of clothes that once was the third man had been almost totally absorbed into the machine, much like the detached arm some months previous.

We sat at the kitchen table sipping from glasses frosted by the cold, filtered water. We looked at each other, and without a word decided that today was the day to try and talk to them again. We had discussed it many times. It was easy to approach them once our decision was made.

"Umm... hi," I said.

The two men did not move. The two men did nothing to show that they had even heard me.

"Umm... hi?" my girlfriend said.

The two men did not move. The two men showed no sign of having heard either me or my girlfriend.

"Well... the thing is, we're worried about you guys. The apartment used to be nice and vibrate-y. We had that lovely blue light to wake up to. We had you three – two – working away at the machine. Now, well, now it just seems sad. It seems like you gave up," I said.

The two men did not stir.

"Can you hear us?" my girlfriend asked.

The two men did not react.

"Can we help? Would you like some water or food?" I asked.

The two men did not answer.

My girlfriend stood up and approached the one-armed man.

"Wait," I yelped, "don't touch him! We keep breaking them!"

"I know. That's why I was going for the one armed one. I thought I could try and rouse him by shaking the shoulder of the missing arm. You know, sort of minimize possible damage?"

"Oh... yes... that's probably a good plan. Be careful," I said pointlessly. I knew that she would always be careful.

She reached out her hand and touched the one-armed man on the shoulder.

"Sir?"

He did not respond.

She looked to me, her hand resting gently on him.

I nodded.

She, ever so gently, shook his shoulder.

The man with one arm collapsed into dust and uniform.

"Oh no!" she yelled as she scooted away from the dust and empty cloth.

I reached out and grasped her arm gently. It was warm and firm. She twisted to look over her shoulder at me. Her eyes looked so sad. I lifted her shirt collar over her mouth.

"Just to be safe, for the baby. I have no idea what those guys are made of."

"That's smart," she said in a voice trembling on the verge of tears.

"Oh, honey, please don't be sad. I should have tried to rouse them. This wasn't your fault! These things happen. There was nothing we could do!" I tried to calm her.

"Oh no," she wept, "I know... I know... but they were so kind, so delicate."

"They were," I agreed. "There's still one left, and the machine."

"What do we do?" she asked. "He looks like the other two before they crumbled. And the machine is silent!"

"We should try and water him. They went dusty. Maybe some water would help. The blood helped the machine. Maybe some water or blood could help?"

My girlfriend agreed with me. She stood up and got the filtered carafe of cold water from the refrigerator. She sat down next to me at the table. The water in the carafe shook from her nervous hand.

"I'll do it," I said.

She smiled and nodded. Her eyes were red and watery.

I took the carafe of cold, filtered, water into my hand and stood. The blue blanket, and the last man, were motionless. I stepped over to him. I made visible signs in front of his eyes that I was going to try and give him water. He showed no signs of understanding.

I touched his chin as gently as I could. His eyes remained open, still and unseeing. I tipped his chin back and was pleasantly surprised that he did not go to dust. I lightly parted his lips and was happy that he did not go to dust. I lifted the carafe of cold, filtered, water to his lips. I poured a small amount of water into his mouth. I heard my girlfriend gasp before I saw what startled her. The last man on a blue blanket on my kitchen floor was leaking from his lower back. He was turning to a mass of foaming gray bubbles. I stopped pouring water immediately, but it was too late. He collapsed into a pile of wet, muddy cloth.

I stood up and took in the scene.

The blanket held a machine that looked like a city.

On the blanket a triangle was marked: one point a wet pile of mud and cloth; one point a uniform covered in dust; on the last, a cloud of dust settling slowly down.

"Does this mean it's finished?" she asked.

"I don't know. It would be sad if they all went to dust before it was completed."

My girlfriend held me from the side. I held her in return. The three men in my kitchen no longer were three men. They were disintegrated, gone. Only their work remained, though silent, lifeless.

———————————————————

The next year we, my girlfriend, our child, and I, were sitting on the floor in front of the couch. Our baby was fat and happy. We were young and happy. Her crib sat in the corner as we played on the floor. My wife smiled at me when we felt the floor. A subtle hum was emanating from the corner of a blue blanket hanging from the crib. Our baby giggled as the apartment turned a pale, familiar blue.

THE
BOOK OF LISTS

1. East of Portland

It was many years ago.

So many in fact that it's hard to remember who we were at the time.

It was many years ago. We had read a story about a store that specialized in things that were lost, a store of lost objects, of forgotten concepts. The idea fascinated us. We longed to visit the store of lost things – of missing friends; of lost lighters; of long-lost curios, rings, baubles, necklaces, and long forgotten aspects of self. It was supposed to be located in some small East Coast town, nameless, locationless, achingly close to a reality in which we could exist. We followed clues. We asked other readers. More than once, we planned the trip. We imagined plane flights, and rental cars. We whispered about making love in small motel rooms along the path of the great journey to the place of lost things. In our free moments we'd think about the things we'd want back. And, in the end, we both made lists of the items we'd find in the place of lost things.

Her list:

1. Stuffed tiger from childhood (Benny)

2. The comfy boots she left in a hotel in Florida

3. The cat from our old house (Pancake)

4. The rock and coin "collection" in the rotten shoebox

5. A raw sense of wonder

6. The ever-summer of youth

My list:

1. The rusty key that I kept on the shelf of weird things

2. The drawings my friend, long dead, made me

3. The ancient tarot deck in the attic

4. My old poems that died in a hard drive failure

5. The easy joy I lost when things began to go wrong

We decided that these would be easily found at the store of lost things. And so we dreamed of the trip. And so we lived for those years, until a drunk man driving a truck slammed into her car. She died instantly. We buried her along with a silly bracelet I bought her when we first got together. It was pink and made of cheap plastic. It was a talisman. I added that bracelet to my list, directly over her name, the paper bubbled in the spots of dried tears.

2. *The lonely journey across desolate country*

I left the city of Portland as a diminishing image in a poorly situated rearview mirror stuck to the window of a rapidly aging Honda. The Honda was once blue, and I was headed east with a vague notion of New York in my mind. By the time the lush green of western Oregon had turned to the desert east, the music from the speakers had hit a sweet spot. The sound of tires on road added the backing track, lulling me into a blissful, mindless road-hypnosis. The mile markers passed by unnoticed as I tried to silence the frequent aching reminders that she was gone. Every song reminded me of her. Every bit of silence reminded me of her. My only reprieves were the periods of hypnosis, the moments where I didn't so much forget as didn't actively ache with reminders of what was gone.

I was nearing the Idaho border when I decided to stop for the night. The landscape was different enough from where I started to give me hope that less of the world would send me spinning with memories and the horrors that they brought.

The motel was a single-story U-shaped complex. A dull-pink vacancy sign blinked over the head of the man behind the desk at the center of the U. He looked to be in his mid-50s, unremarkable in every aspect. His eyes, fixed to a television hanging from the ceiling, were a dull, unintelligent brown. He looked like his life had ended decades ago, but his body continued on with his work- an automated corpse at the desk of Motel Nameless.

The man behind the desk gave me my door key on a loop with a tattered laminated tag reading '#12.' I thanked him and went into my room. It was small with little decoration, but shockingly tidy. The table tops, mirrors, and carpet looked new or freshly cleaned. I thought that I might have misread the man behind the desk. This room showed that someone cared enough to keep the place neat and organized. Or, I then thought, that he might not have anything to do with the cleaning. I suppose that a solitary man sitting bored behind the counter of a small motel at 10pm on a Tuesday probably isn't in charge of much besides his counter. I left my bag of clothes and toiletries in the room and left, pocketing the disintegrating #12 laminate.

I asked the man at the counter if he knew where I could get a drink. He, not taking his eyes off the television, told me to walk three blocks north to the local bar. I asked him which way was north. He sighed and told me to make a left out of the office door. I thanked him again and walked out, making the aforementioned left.

The place where I could get a drink turned out to be a bar called "The Tankard." It was a solitary red brick building with a broken neon sign. I entered through the battered oak front door. The bar was dimly lit, sparsely populated, and quiet as a grave. It was perfect.

I walked across a room full of empty tables and sat down at the bar. The stools were the perfect height to allow my feet to rest on the foot rail. I was pleased by this. I asked the bartender for a pint of the cheap and a shot of whiskey. He was confused by my phrasing. Rearranging my words, I requested whatever inexpensive beer he had on tap and a shot of whiskey. He poured my beer and whiskey and left me to my own devices. I liked that bar. It allowed me to be alone, yet in public. I watched the few patrons in the mirror behind the bar. They all looked like me: sullen, tired, bored. The room filled up a bit as the night continued on.

A group of five men and women, all somewhere in their twenties, entered and took a table. They spoke too loudly for the room. One, or all of them, noticed their loudness and put money in the jukebox. I liked seeing people who are aware of their surroundings. The first song up was a Tom Waits number from his early work, back when his voice didn't sound like a dirty air filter. I didn't know that young people still listened to Tom Waits. I was at least five years older than all of them. The age gap felt like decades.

The evening continued. People came and left. I scribbled on a notebook that I kept in my pocket. The whiskey made things more tolerable. The throbbing ache of my life at that time was dulled to the point of ignorability.

One of the girls from the table of people in their mid-20s walked past me, presumably to the bathroom. We made sheepish eye contact, which I broke as quickly as possible. She was young and beautiful. I was aging and broken. I thought about her for a few minutes until I was interrupted by that same woman sitting at my right.

"How are you?" she asked.

I thought about this. I never know how to answer that question, even when I was in a better place. Did they really mean to ask about my actual mood? Were they simply using that phrase as a form of hello? I don't like lying; so saying 'I'm okay' felt wrong. After too long of a moment, for I saw her grow uncomfortable, I answered.

"I'm not well at all," I said. "My life imploded recently and I have no idea how to continue on."

"Oh," she said.

"Sorry, I never know how to answer people when they ask how

I am. Even if I were to be in a good mood, it feels awkward, fake, to say 'I'm good.' Do you know what I mean?"

She stared at me. She was pretty. Her eyes were soft and looked like they could offer immense comfort to those in her sphere.

"I think I know what you mean," she said, thoughtfully. "You like to tell the truth. I guess people don't like to hear the truth for the most part, right?"

"Yes. Something very close to that," I said. "I feel, frankly, terrible. Saying that makes things weird... But I don't want to start an interaction with a lie. So when I'm asked how I am, I never know how to answer."

She smiled. She had a very genuine, lovely smile. It lit her face. She glowed.

"You're a good man," she said, touching my hand with hers. "You should sit with us."

"Oh... well, I sorta like being alone," I said.

"You said sorta. That makes me think, since you're honest, that there's a part of you that would like some company."

I paused for slightly longer than she seemed comfortable with.

"Hmm... I think you're right. If you're genuine about the request, I think that I would like to sit with you and your friends."

"The request was genuine," she said. "Do you need a refill first, or shall we head over?"

"I'm ok for the moment," I said, standing.

"Wait, what's your name? My name is ██████."

"Of course it is," I said, sardonically. "I'm Thomas."

"Of course it is?"

"Sorry, didn't mean to say that out loud. It's just that your name was recently in my life. No fault of your own."

"I understand."

Something about the way she said it made me think that she may just have.

She took my hand, the one without a beer, and lead me over to her table.

After a brief round of ineffective introductions, I sat down. All their names bled into the background noise of clinking glass and unexpected song choices. Her friends were talking about a mountain they had climbed. I didn't catch its name. The far-too-handsome young man at my left was giving a rousing recital of the moment he saw the sun crest over the horizon as he sat on a ledge near the peak. He made it sound beautiful. The woman across from me was also very attractive. She smiled and told us that she knows that feeling as well. I realized that I was, by far, the least interesting person at the table. To be fair though, I generally think this anyway. I struggle to understand why anyone would choose to spend their time with me. I asked ▮▮▮▮ this once. She told me in a very sweet and simple voice, as if she were talking to child, that I was interesting. She said that I was just bored of my stories. I thought that was a reasonable line of thinking. But I had never climbed a mountain to see the glowing dawn horizon, and therefore felt socially inadequate.

"Thomas, what brings you out here?" ▮▮▮▮ asked.

The group all looked at me as I paused in thought.

"Well... I guess..." I vacillated between telling the whole truth or some edited version. "Do you want the real story, which is horrible, or should I edit?"

"Whatever you're comfortable with," The handsome man

across from me said.

His companions agreed. ▇▇▇ placed her hand gently on mine and smiled sympathetically.

"Okay, I'll give it a shot. I'm driving East at the moment." I said.

"Why are you doing that?" The pretty, nameless lady asked.

"I had a notion that there's something to be found in New York, or Connecticut... not sure exactly where it is," I said.

"Any reason, or just a vacation?" Handsome-Man asked.

I swallowed and gripped my beer.

"Well... until very recently I had a long-term girlfriend," I said with a shaking voice. "I was sure we were going to spend the rest of our lives together. I was half right. So now I'm alone and have no idea what to do with my life. I have no idea how to live without... without her... so... yeah... driving."

A weighted, uncomfortable pause followed my statement. I stared into my drink, rubbing the glass with my finger.

▇▇▇ held my hand and said, "I'm so sorry."

Her friends nodded and mumbled their solemn agreements.

"What's in New York?" The other nameless lady asked.

"We found this story... place... something," I said, thinking this was impossible to explain. "In that story the place sells forgotten and lost things. You know, like trinkets and whatever you lost over the years. ▇▇▇ and I... her name was ▇▇▇... well, we made up lists of the things we'd like to get back if we found the store. I couldn't think of anything else to do after... well... after. So I'm driving east to find a store of forgotten and lost things. I have both our lists still... and... well... yeah... east."

There was a rather pregnant pause. Some of them took

uncomfortable sips of beer. I followed suit. I noticed that my hand was shaking. The scene was blurring as if seen through water. A drop exploded on the table directly under my head.

"Excuse me, sorry, just need the restroom," I said.

I got up without hearing their responses, and walked to the bathroom. I grabbed the sink with both hands, my knuckles white with effort, and looked into the mirror. My eyes were red, but not so bad as to be noticeable. I needed a shave. But overall I still looked like myself. It was good to see that I didn't look like I felt. I splashed water on my face and dried it with paper towels. I could smell the wet paper under my nose as I walked back to the table.

"Hey there!" ████ yipped. "We're making our lists."

"Your lists?" I asked, confused.

"Yes, our lists," said Handsome-Man. "We thought that your story was incredible. So we're making our lists in case we ever find your place of forgotten things."

I smiled like an idiot. They understood our idea.

"That's great," I said. "What do you have so far?"

"I came up with three!" the third woman, who had previously just listened, said. "Want to hear them?"

"Yes, I'd love to."

She beamed.

"Well, number one is this really old arcade token I had from when I went to a beachfront pinball place with my parents. I kept that token forever, but it got lost when I moved away from home."

"That's a really great one. If I had that story in my head, I'd like to get my token back as well."

"Thanks!" she said brightly. "Next, and I'm not sure if this counts, I'd like to get back the puppy I had when I was a kid. She was so cute and fun. But that might be cheating."

"That's not cheating. It counts," I said definitively. "█████ wanted a cat back. We discussed it at length and decided that the store of forgotten things had the ability to sell lost animals as well. So your puppy idea is a good one."

She bounced in her seat and grinned.

"Perfect! That puppy was great. The third thing I came up with was... and this is kind of stupid. But I'd want to get my virginity back."

The table giggled. She looked embarrassed.

"It's not that I want to be a virgin now!" she exclaimed too loudly. "It's just that the first guy was a jerk. I'd like to get that one back and let the second guy be my first. I think I'd like my life a little better if that was how it happened."

"Sorry to laugh," Less-Handsome-Man said. "It's a sweet idea. I was only laughing because I got uncomfortable. I'm an idiot."

"It's okay," she said. "I don't mind. It's kinda silly."

"I loved it." I said. "Anyone else have any?"

"Actually," Less-Handsome-Man interjected. "I laughed because mine is really stupid and might sound terrible."

"It's just a list," I said. "We won't find you terrible.

"Well... I'd like..." he stammered. "Not for what you think... but I'd like my old computer back. I had... umm... personal pictures on there. God, I sound like a creep... but it would, I don't know, remind me of where I came from to see them again... Ugh... I can't believe I said that out loud."

"It's okay," I said quickly. "Nothing included on any list should be a cause for shame. It's sorta an unofficial rule to the whole concept."

"Thanks," he said, mollified. "I really hope you guys don't think I'm a creep. It's not really sexual... it's, like, lost intimacy or something."

"You're not a creep," Quiet-Girl said. "I get it."

We sat for a minute. They all seemed comfortable in the silence. I guessed that they had known each other for a long time. They were accustomed to being around each other, even during the awkward pauses.

"I only came up with one," ████ said. "I had this toy I called Gilly when I was a little girl. It was some kind of stuffed thing with an odd pointy hat. I loved that stupid thing. I have no idea where it went. Hell, I'd buy one on eBay if I knew the actual name of the toy."

"That's nice," I said. "I hope you find Gilly."

"Thanks!" she said. "But I'm okay with simply wanting her. What would I do with Gilly if I found her? I'm 28 and have no kids. After the initial excitement of finding it, I'm sure I'd get bored. In a way it's nicer to stay in want, actually."

"Hmm..." I said. "I think you're right."

"I have one," said Handsome-Man. "I had a cigar box that my grandfather gave me. I filled it with stupid little kid stuff. I'd love to have that back, even for a night. I'm really curious what the little kid version of me would want to keep."

"You nearly made a list when you were little," I said. "'The list of things I'd rather not lose.' That's great."

"Thanks," he said.

He gave a strange smile. It looked more real than the plastic, handsome, smile he'd used before. I began to think that I had misread him.

We sat in silence for a moment. I sipped from my beer. The others looked around nervously. I had a feeling that something was not being said.

Less-Handsome-Man got up to get us another round of drinks. We waited, tapping the table to a Leonard Cohen song. I assumed it was chosen by my table. He finally returned with a tray of various sized glasses.

"Cheers," he said, raising his drink."

We all returned the motion in kind.

"So, Thomas," ███ said hesitantly. "Can we ask about your list? Please don't share if you don't want to... but I think we're all curious."

"Yeah," the rest of the table said in near unison.

"Okay... sure," I said as I pulled out my wallet. I took out a folded piece of paper from an inner pocket and neatly unfolded it. "It goes like this..."

I read them my list. I paused between each item for interjections, but no one spoke. I finished my five items, the items from when she was alive. The later additions were left silent. The later additions were only for me. I refolded the paper and put it carefully back into my wallet. It was only a copy, but I treated it with respect.

"That was a good list," Quiet-Girl said.

"Yeah," Handsome-Man said.

"..." Less-Handsome-Man said.

"Thank you, Thomas," said ███. "That couldn't have been easy."

"Thank you guys... I thought I wanted to be alone when I came in... but this is nice. I really appreciate it."

After I finished saying it I realized that I meant it. I needed a break – even this small one – from the unremitting pain of her loss.

We spent the rest of the evening chatting and, eventually, singing along to the juke box. I told them I was surprised by their choices in music. They chided me about being way too old for my age. They were right. I've been old since I was a little kid. I ended up introducing them to a few bands they didn't know. They responded in kind. It was a pleasant evening that I desperately needed. The stabbing horror within me was dulled as we spent hours being real, functioning people.

As the night progressed, they told me of their lives and travels. They were from Portland as well, but had been based out of Idaho for the last few months on various adventures. They said that they had a house a few miles away and that I was welcome to stay there. I thanked them, but said that I wanted to use my motel room since I was leaving early and all my stuff was in there. They jokingly begged me to stay. I responded as best I could. The bartender signaled last call, so I got a shot of whiskey for the road. I was predicting poor sleep. A night of lessened pain felt like an invitation to a late night of weeping insomnia.

I took my shot at the bar and paid the rest of my tab. ▮▮▮▮ sat next to me.

"I want to sleep with you," she said, directly.

I was not expecting that. I didn't respond.

"Shit... sorry," she said.

It was the first swear I heard her use. She sounded awkward using it.

"What I meant to say is, I want to go to your hotel with you and lay next to you... I want to hold you as much as you'll let me. Nothing sexual... I can't go home knowing you're alone in that motel. I can't let you leave us like that. Please?"

I could hear the hum of the bar's refrigerator in the gulf of silence. I didn't know what to say. I wasn't expecting anything like that to happen. It hadn't occurred to me that there could be someone else in the universe who would want to stay near me.

"Umm..." I said. It was all I could think of.

"Look, Thomas," she said. "I think I understand you. And please believe me when I tell you that this is better. You have an entire lonely country ahead of you, please let me be your friend tonight."

"Umm..." I said. "I don't know... I'm no good at this stuff. This is a real offer, no weirdness?"

"I swear to you that I just want to share a bed," she said touching my shoulder.

"What about your friends?"

"They're fine. We don't have plans tomorrow or anything. So, how about you let a pretty girl hug you?" she smirked.

I paused. This was nothing I was used to.

"Umm... yeah, that would be nice," I said, my voice faltering.

"Good, wait here."

She jogged to her friends. She didn't stagger or lose a step. That made me comfortable. I didn't want to think this was a drunken thing. If I were honest with myself, I wouldn't have minded if it were only a drunken thing. I wanted a warm body near me. I wanted to feel better, if only for a few hours.

Her hand was on my shoulder. I was looking at her in the mirror behind the bar.

"Ready to go?" she said, resolutely.

"Sure," I said. "Sorry to keep asking, but are you sure about this? This sort of thing isn't common to me."

"Everything is perfect and as it should be," she said. "Now shut up and walk with me."

Her smile was perfect and warm. She was a singular moment made flesh. I had no idea what I was doing. We walked to my motel. I saw through the window the clerk sleeping in his chair as we passed. He had a good job. I opened the door with the key hanging from the #12 laminate. We entered and turned on lights.

"Oh... this place is clean! I never would have guessed!"

"Yeah, I thought the same thing. I'm glad I chose to stop here." I said, a light smile on my lips.

"Me too. I'm very glad we found each other, Thomas."

We sat on the bed and watched TV for a bit. She stroked my back and my hair. It was lovely. I began to nod, and she ordered me to get ready for bed. We had an awkward conversation about proper sleeping attire. It was decided that she would leave on bra and panties and wear one of my shirts. Everything was covered and proper. I wore boxers and an undershirt. She walked across the room in near darkness and climbed into bed with me. I was on my back and she shimmied up as close as could be allowed. Her leg bent across my thighs. Her face in the crook of my neck. I could feel her breasts pressed against my ribs. I felt my erection grow. Her leg moved and hit it.

"Sorry," I said. "Just a chemical thing, I swear."

"It's okay," she said. "I understand."

She lightly kissed my cheek.

"Thomas, I really am sorry for what you've gone through."

There was a long pause.

"But I'm glad that you ended up here. I'm glad that I found you."

"Me too," I said. "Thank you."

We eventually fell asleep, entwined.

Hours later, I woke up with her hair under my nose. It smelled of flowers and stale beer. I rubbed her back with my free arm and felt very thankful. I looked at the ceiling of my motel room, creating vague constellations from the bumps in the plaster. Her breath was hot on my chest. I felt bad for how comfortable I felt.

Why did this happen now when it was impossible? Why was I completely broken when I met this lovely woman? I came up with no answers. The bumpy plaster zodiac gave no insights. I laid in my terrible bed and felt the chasm within me open again. The familiar ████-shaped hole beginning to throb in the morning light. The call of the east still screamed within me, but it could be put off, just for a bit, just till she woke, just till I took in the last moments with a person of such perfect compassion. And in feeling her compassion I felt even worse. How could I allow myself comfort when she was moldering in the ground? How could I betray ████ by letting myself hold this strange woman who so brazenly shared her name. How dare I feel comfort when she would never feel anything again?

I extracted my arm, numb from blood loss, from under ████. I decided to shower instead of lying in bed attempting to parse that combination of heartbreak and comfort. In the shower a man can think – or not if need be. It is his domain to use as is his whim. My whim was to scrub my hair with terrible motel shampoo and weep. By the time I was dry and dressed I felt like I could attempt some rational thought. I walked back into the room and the empty bed therein. I stood in place and focused on the rightmost pillow. It still held an indent. It proved she existed. It proved there was a woman of such empathy as to mark a pillow with her head. It proved that there was such grace in the universe that the previous night could have happened. It proved she existed, at least for those hours when I was in such need that I could not have named a method to sate it. She existed. She, with her name, existed. I still existed, alone in a motel room with a ██████-shaped hole. It was nearly Idaho and I was about to start driving East again. There was a note on the dresser stand. My heart skipped. Finally, I would get that goodbye I so desperately needed.

Thomas,

This is my list. It is not for forgotten things. Please read it in good health.
1) The moment I saw your eyes. They are soft and articulate.
2) How your voice trembles when you say her name.
3) How your voice sounds strong when you say mine.
4) Your apologies for everything.
5) Your heart, and my belief that it will heal.

I could have loved you. I think you could have loved me. This was perfect. I am a better person for our time together. Please find your place of forgotten things. Please find the healing and solace you so desperately deserve. Please keep safe as you move east. If you ever find yourself in the NW again, find me. I know you will thrive after the coming months.

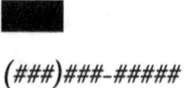
It was a perfect note. I folded it up and slipped it into my wallet, mentally taking a note to make a copy so I don't lose the original. I packed up the loose odds and ends of the motel room and checked out. There was a different man behind the counter, dressed in a nice-looking suit. He didn't look as interesting as my friend from last night. Maybe he was the owner. I gave him the key on its peeling laminate. The motel grew ever smaller in my rear-view mirror.

3. *Montana and the things held therein*

When I crossed the border into Idaho I was struck by how much it looked like Eastern Oregon. This shouldn't have struck me as odd, given that the only difference between the two areas is a man-made border invisible save for the "Welcome to..." sign, so I kept driving. It was a nice enough drive. I found a radio station that had a man talking about beekeeping. I thought about the word "apiary" for close to 100 miles. That day moved by in a blur of highways and gas stations. It moved at the pace of bad food and worse coffee. I was somewhere in Montana when I decided to stop for the night. The air smelled amazing. The chain-motel was completely forgettable, soulless, but reasonably clean. The woman behind the counter looked like everyone at once. Her face was a pastiche of faces from 28 to 42 years old. She was pleasant and incredibly forgettable. She handed me a key hanging from a plastic tag inscribed with #12. I found it odd that

I was in #12 again. The room looked nothing like my last #12. It had a sense of perpetual uncleanliness, just short of actually dirty. I dropped my bag off and brushed my teeth. I locked the door behind me and walked back to the desk. I could hear the tenants upstairs howling wildly. I wished that I could enjoy life that much. I lamented my lack of desire to howl in joy.

The pastiche-faced woman told me that the bar next door was okay. She made sure to mention that no one would mess with me there. That did not give me hope for my stay in Montana. I walked to the bar next door. It was called Bruce's or Kevin's or some other equally unoriginal name. It was nearly as forgettable as Pastiche-Face.

The bar's interior looked like a suburban basement from the 1970s. The seats were black Naugahyde. The walls were striped with carpeting in black and dark red interrupted by mounted heads of various animals. Everything was either dusty or dulled by age. The crescent shaped bar was populated by a few faceless men watching sports on an old cathode tube TV. I sat as far from the men and the TV as possible. I caught the eye of the bartender who wore an ancient cowboy hat, a dull blue shirt, and way too-tight blue jeans. I ordered a beer with a shot, and he nodded with a grunt. There's something very comforting about a bartender who only nods and grunts. That's the kind of man who knows how to handle himself. Or so it appeared to me. He placed the drinks down with paradoxical gentility. I thanked him and left a few bucks for a tip. He seemed the type to favor good tippers with more frequent attention and larger shots. I was proven correct over the next few hours.

No one spoke at that bar. It was nice at first. But as the night continued it grew uncomfortable. I supposed that everyone was a regular, so communication wasn't needed for the most part. Each drink poured was received with a silent nod from the drinker. I felt even more out of place with each silent refill. I started to see what the forgettable lady at the motel meant by "no one would mess with you." No one messed, interacted, or talked with anyone. It was a bar of willing mutes. It was an alcohol monastery, sanctified by vows of silence. I was transgressing in their church. I was a non-believer in that most holy place. I stared into my whiskey and tried to fit in. It wasn't hard. I pictured ███ lying dead under the earth. Her body would probably still be perfect, formaldehyde keeping back the decay. I hated those thoughts. They were intruders upon my moments of lessened pain. So I drank in that silent seminary until my eyes blurred. I walked back to the motel bed alone and slightly unstable. The darkness of the room engulfed me as I curled up in the mold-smelling bed, crying desperate, lonely, tears.

The next day I spent in bed, hungover, listless. The room was always slightly too warm or slightly too cold. The activities of the day were limited to adjusting the thermostat; napping; eating horrible vending machine food; and watching endless, attentionless TV. It was nearing 8pm when I decided to shower and leave my room. The Montana sky hit me in the face with a blast of stars cradled in sweet, cool air. I walked to the bar with the forgettable name. I had a book with me. I felt that they wouldn't mind a reader using up a corner seat so long as that reader drank frequently and in quiet.

The bar was exactly as it was the night before... exactly. The same seats were taken by the same men. The same bartender waited for me to order. His nods and grunts showed no sign of recognition. I drank in quiet anonymity in the nameless bar until the words of my book grew indistinct.

I stumbled back to the motel under the blurred and shifting stars. I felt tears forming, yet again. I walked towards my room sobbing deeply. The room above mine was making lots of noise, ashing cigarettes over the railing. One of them called out to me to join in the revelry. I ignored him and wobbled my way into my room instead. The bathroom was too bright. I tried to vomit, but all that was left in me was bile. I crawled to my bed hoping I'd find real food to eat in the morning. The morning arrived with an aching head screaming for water. The slightly brown tap water was good enough for that moment. My head spun as I leaned over the sink drinking deeply from the running faucet. It was nearly two hours before I felt like a person again. I had missed checkout yet again, so I paid for another night at the utterly forgettable chain motel. The clerk, this time a squat, round man, told me of the local attractions. One was an easy hike up a "mountain" about 20 miles away. I thought a hike would be perfect, so I pointed my car towards the easy mountain. One pit-stop at a pancake shop later and I was full of coffee and starch, ready for the climb.

There was no climb, per se. There was, however, a parking lot on a steep hill. After a half hour walk I had reached the trail to the summit. I was glad the hike was so short; I was still a little hungover. It was 54 minutes from the parking lot when I crossed the boundary between woods and viewpoint. It was stunning. The land rolled out from my mountain as if it were the origin of all things. It spread itself out into the nothing as if it were Eden reborn. And it was, for that moment, Eden, the point of all creation. This mountain looked out over us like a loving creator, like a parent just out of sight. My heart ached. My head swam with the immensity of it. I sat down on a patch of grass and watched nothing in particular. I cried more than once during my mountaintop vigil. I laughed more than once as I sat in a broken lotus position. I was a destroyed Buddha in a crumbling shrine, a faithless man wandering through sacred temples. I was watching the world and it was empty, void. I was universal consciousness, and there was nothing in the universe. I watched the sun set into a pale peach glow before I tried to stand again. My legs were numb, nearly useless. I tried to rub some sensation back into them. My filthy hands, darkened through unconscious grasping of earth, dirtied the pale blue of my jeans as blood once again began to flow. I walked down the path to my car by the scattered light of stars and the occasional flashlight app on my phone. I managed it uninjured. I sat in the dark car and looked at the trees. I had no desire to do anything anymore. I wanted to turn everything off, to fall into some dark place and be forgotten. My eyes grew heavy. I didn't want to drive to my motel. The front seat reclined, taking me with it. The air in the car grew stale as the night passed.

Dawn hit my window like a fire. I shook my head and tried to remember where I was. I had no idea where I was, where I was going, or where I had been. I had a motel key which worked. I had a car which worked. I used those as a compass, returning to my terrible nightly home. The pastiche woman was back at the counter when I arrived. She nodded at me. I felt, somehow, that she understood. She, the amalgamated woman, would understand me, the directionless man.

I spent the day listlessly watching the television. I reread the three lists I had with me, searching for a clue. The hours crawled. I used the motel laundry. I used my shower. The hours crawled. I walked back to the nameless bar.

The same men sat in the same places. The bartender stood as still as statuary. A few of the same men had slightly different faces. I took "my" seat and ordered a cheap beer and shot. The bartender grunted and shuffled away to fetch my drinks. The glasses thunked down on the bar, and he spoke.

"You live here now or something?"

His voice was softer, higher, than I expected. But it was a gentle voice; a slight cigarette rasp hinted at the edges. It was nice.

"Oh, me?" I asked, stupidly.

"Yeah, you. You've been in here lately. We don't see many new faces make a second appearance... Once you're here three times, seems to me that you might be here to stay."

"I dunno. I'm staying at the hotel across the way for now. I'm heading east... or was. Kinda got stuck."

"Huh," he grunted. "I hope you don't. You're too young for this shit."

He gestured to indicate the breadth of the bar.

"It doesn't seem so bad. It's comfortable. Nice area. Walked up the mountain yesterday."

"..." he grunted. "It's a good joint to end at. Go east. Meet girls. Be young."

"Thanks," I said. "I appreciate that."

He grunted a nod and walked back to the other side of the bar. I drank quietly and tried to picture getting back on the road. It seemed like the right idea.

I left after that round, saying goodbye to the bartender. He nodded and twitched his hand in what could have been a wave goodbye.

The nameless bar was left in my rear-view the next morning.

I played no music in honor of it having existed.

4. *The square states somewhere in the middle*

Wyoming.

I have almost no memory of being in Wyoming besides my slight embarrassment at realizing there wasn't an 'h' after the 'W'. I was far too old to misspell the names of states. I passed through some form of Dakota or another in a haze of dreary boredom. All the energy from Idaho was long gone. The days in Montana were quickly receding into vague memories of feeling horrible. The idea of being on the east coast and finding a mystical place of lost things seemed stupid. I just wanted to go home and sleep. The problem was that I had nowhere to call home. Portland was a chasm, a devouring vortex of pain and memories of her. I had nothing better to do than press forward into the depths of the eastern night. I drove with a bored determination, a listless ennui transmuted into eastward momentum.

The radio pulsed in and out of my consciousness, in and out of tune. It was, at times, a friend. It was, at times, no different from the dull drone of tires on asphalt. I was rounding a curve on a twisting local route when the radio, with no compassion, stabbed me. I didn't notice the opening of the song. I should have. Or maybe not – I would have changed the station immediately if I had. I only noticed that the song was playing when the knife of lyrics entered my chest. It was THE song. It was HER song. I barely managed to pull the car to the side of the road before my eyes were blurred my body racked with spasms of agony. That song, even when she was alive, made me lonesome for her, even if I knew I'd see her in a few hours. That was her song, totemic as anything that may be sitting on a dusty shelf in a place of forgotten things. It was her song, and it was killing me. I cried for a long time after it ended. My throat felt raw. My face was a puffy, red mess. Eternities passed as I finally got my breathing under control. I wiped my face with hands stiff from squeezing misery-filled fists. I don't remember the next song, or the next. I was almost myself again when the radio went back in for seconds.

I heard the opening bars to the song we used to sing together at the top of our lungs when we were giddy from booze or long car rides. I started to cry again, until the chorus hit. It was so stupid. It was such a stupid song. And I started to laugh. It felt as if my ████-shaped hole had contracted, that I was spewing up some of that pain. And I laughed louder. And when the chorus circled back around I leaned back on the seat, threw back my head and screamed along at the top of my lungs. I felt, for a second, like a person again. I felt, for a second, like who I was when I was with her. As the song faded out to the clicking of my turn signal, I got back on the road. The radio was clear. The rumble of the pavement felt something like comfort.

5. The art scene is great in Minnesota

Three days of driving from greasy diners to dirty motels later, I entered Minnesota. I was somewhat excited to be in Minnesota. I had heard of places there. There was something called the Twin Cities, and possibly it was where Bob Dylan came from. I found the Twin Cities. I did not find Bob Dylan. St. Paul was better for no particular reason. The air simply felt friendlier to my lungs. So I left my car at some cut-rate hotel and walked around. I stumbled on a kind of art-district.

████ was the art fan. I certainly enjoyed looking at paintings with her, but I was never one to go alone.

There was a small block of stores next to a street that I assumed was an important inner-city artery. The small block housed a line of galleries, studios, fancy cafés, and all the other signs of a creative district. I looked through the window of one such café and saw that the walls were covered in framed charcoal drawings. Something about the charcoal lines attracted me, drew me into the small coffee shop. It was warm. The floor was covered in tables and chairs of various shapes and mismatched sizes. It looked comfortable. It looked real.

I got a coffee from the nice-looking lady behind the counter and slowly started to pace the room, taking in the drawings. They were, in a word, perfect. The charcoal lines, all fading at the edges, moved frenetically from the center out. They looked like life in decay. They were full of desperation, of a broken person searching for meaning, for healing. They were like a visual guide to my life since the accident. I sipped my coffee midway through the first wall. It was stone cold. I walked back to the counter and asked for another.

"Want me to warm this one up a touch?" She asked. "Looks like you didn't touch it."

"Sorry, I just…" I paused. "The art. It's… it's… I don't know art words. It's effective? I fell in… Jesus, sorry. Yeah, a warm up would be lovely. Thanks so much."

"No problem," she answered, handing his cup back. "Please enjoy the art."

"I will. Thanks."

I paced the coffee shop for close to two hours taking in the drawings. The next time my cup went cold the girl behind the counter told me I didn't need to buy anything to look at the art. She was very nice. When I finished the last wall I went back to the counter.

"I really like them. I never do this sort of thing."

"That's perfectly cool. That's why we hang art. Hopefully it strikes someone's fancy, or at least makes them think."

"It does both," I said. "I feel like if I could make art I'd try to make these... or, I dunno, try to communicate something like they're communicating... does that make sense? I don't know proper art language."

"It makes complete sense. I'm sure the artist would like that. What brings you here? I don't recall your face."

"It's my first time in St. Paul. I don't know what brought me here, to be honest. I was wandering around and looked in."

"Where are you from?"

"Portland... the Oregon one."

"Oh yeah?" she asked. "Is it as amazing as we keep hearing?"

"Hah, no. It's just a city. But I don't really live there anymore. I guess I don't live anywhere right now..." I noticed her look slightly worried. "Oh, I'm not homeless... well, I mean, I am. But it's my choice. I gave up my apartment and belongings and am driving East. I'll get a permanent address once I decide where I'd like to stop."

"Wow. That's pretty brave. Good job."

"Thanks... it isn't so much brave as, well, the other." I swallowed with a dry throat. "I couldn't stay there anymore. Bad memories, you know?"

"I think I understand," she smiled, making a deep, soft eye contact. "How long are you in town?"

"No idea. One night... two... the rest of my life? Right now I have my car and a shitty hotel room. No defined plans."

"Well, would you like to get a drink with me after I close? I'd like to hear more of your story."

"Umm... well..." I stammered.

"I'm gay," she interrupted.

"Huh?"

"I'm gay. You were 'umming' like you didn't know how to let a girl hitting on you down gently. I only wanted to chat some more."

"Oh... No, it wasn't that kind of 'umm.' I ummed because you seem nice and I'd like to chat. But that makes me feel uncomfortable these days. I guess I sorta feel like I need to pay penance.... torture myself or something... Oh Jesus I sound like a nutjob, hah! Still want to chat?"

"Oh course! Holy shit man, you can't say tempting stuff like that and think I don't want to know more. How about you meet me outside at 9:15?"

"Sure. I'll see you then."

"See ya, I'm Steph, by the way."

"Thomas. Nice to meet you."

I walked towards where I thought my motel existed. I found it after an hour. There was nothing to do in the room. I don't know why I went back. I suppose it just feels natural to leave for a social engagement from the place you're currently calling home. I napped and I cried. It was such a light round of crying that I felt worse after I finished. I should have wept more heavily, more often. I felt she deserved at least that. She deserved the rending of clothes and painful, dramatic screams into the darkened sky. But all I could muster was a numb, gentle, sob. I let her down often in those days. The walk back to the café was much quicker than I'd expected. It's amazing how much faster direct routes are over confused meandering ones.

The girl from the café was leaning on the wall next to the café trying to look casual. I thought she did a good job of it.

"Hello," I said.

"Hi! I'm glad you showed up."

"Me too," I said, tentatively. "Or is that weird to say? I don't know if this is going to turn out horribly."

"You overthink stuff nearly as much as I do!" she smiled. "Just be glad for right now, then if things go poorly we can adjust our moods accordingly."

"It's a good plan. I'm officially glad I came."

"Let's go, the little lady is waiting."

"The little lady?" I asked.

"My partner. She's meeting us at the place we're going."

"Oh... is that okay? I mean, am I intruding?"

"Nope. I invited you, remember?"

We walked a few blocks away from the river. I never got the hang of which was way north in that city. She stopped us in front of a bar/pub/café/garbage pile. I looked at her as quizzically as I could.

"This is it?"

"Yup," she said smirking. "The inside is better... after a fashion."

The inside was better. In fact, the inside was an exact representation of everything I'd ever want from a pub. It was full of nooks, bookshelves, strange paintings and sculptures, a long dark bar with ancient stools, tables of various sizes, and a tantalizing hallway in the rear promising something more.

"Wow. Good choice," I said.

"Yup. I know my hangout spots. Hey, there she is."

She pointed to a stunningly beautiful woman sitting at the bar- pink hair, huge blue eyes, and radiating skin. She was, quite honestly, the most attractive person I've ever seen in real life.

"Really? Good for you."

"I know, right? I have no idea how I landed that one."

"Seriously, and more importantly, this place has Glenlivet. I haven't had that in months."

"Hey!" She slapped my arm. "My girlfriend is much more attractive than booze!"

"I don't know. They both have their attributes."

"You sure know how to compliment a girl."

"Hey, your partner compares well to a delicious Scotch..."

"What?" The stunning pink-haired woman interrupted.

"He thinks that bottle of Scotch," she said, pointing to the shelves behind the bar, "is more attractive than you."

"Come on, now. I said no such thing. I was simply saying that I'm in dire need of a glass of Scotch. More importantly, you two are in a relationship and I am broken on the inside; the Scotch gets my attention."

"You know, Steph, he has a point," the pink-haired woman said. "I'm going to take it as high praise that someone who is self- proclaimed 'broken' compares me to a good Scotch. I'm smooth and only found in the most respectable of establishments."

"This was a mistake," Steph said in an exaggerated, dramatic voice. "I knew you two would take to each other."

"I'm pretty adorable for an itinerant mess," I said, trying to force as much faux-joy into the words as possible.

"If I were a breeder, I'd hit it," Pink Hair told us.

Steph lightly slapped her arm. They both laughed, then kissed hello. I stood, awkwardly trying to not look awkward.

We ordered drinks and took seats at a horseshoe-shaped couch wrapped around an amoeba-looking table. Steph and her partner with the pink hair said their hellos and check-in questions. They had an easy grace with one another that made me envious. I missed having an easy conversation. I missed the times when I didn't need to bluff my way through pleasant social interactions, hiding my fractures as best I could.

"Anyway, Grace, this little straggler is a new friend of mine, Thomas," she said. "Thomas, this is my partner Grace."

"Nice to meet you."

"You too. By the way, I'm her girlfriend. That 'partner' shit gets on my nerves. There's nothing wrong with "girlfriend" as a term for your part... err, significant other."

"I heard that! You said partner!" Steph said.

"No, I *nearly* said it... the nearly makes all the difference in the world."

"So, how'd you meet my lovely lady?"

"At the café. We got to talking I guess."

"Thomas, tell her a little more about what you were doing there," Steph said.

"I guess I needed to kill some time, so I wandered in. I sorta fell into the art on the walls."

"Oh! Really!" Grace yelped! "That's wonderful, thank you!"

She reached over Steph and tapped my knee.

"...?" I asked.

"Oh Christ, I didn't tell you! I'm an idiot. Sorry Thomas! I got excited. Grace here did all the art that's up this month. That's why I thought you two should meet.

"Really? That's you?" I asked.

"That's me. You actually liked it?"

"Of course."

"Thanks... that means a lot. I don't get to hear from people about my stuff often. It's really gratifying, thanks."

Her giant blue eyes shimmered under the threat the tears.

"They're great. I don't actually know much about art... but something... something about your stuff just... I don't know... dragged me in... it spoke to me maybe? Sorry, I probably sound like an ass."

"You don't," Grace said. "I appreciate it. Those come from a pretty dark place in my life that I've thankfully worked through. It's kinda arrogant to say, but I'm proud of them."

"It's not arrogant. You know that. You're allowed to be proud. You're talented as fuck. We know that." Steph gently placed her arm over Grace's shoulder.

I felt the weight of what must have come before. Her art had helped her heal, was helping her heal. I was watching the last remnants of a traumatic story fade to memory.

"You should be proud. I don't know anything about art. In fact, I've pretty much ignored it all my life. But your work reached me. You're my favorite artist, which was a phrase that sounded much better in my head than aloud." I tried to smile.

Grace looked through me with those incredible eyes.

"Thank you. That's really good to hear. What happened to you?"

"What do you mean?" I asked.

"Well, you've mentioned that you're broken inside; wandering around; and my work spoke to you. It's pretty clear that something went pretty shitty pretty recently in the life of ol' Thomas. So, speak up," Grace insisted, with giant, playfully mocking, smile.

"Grace! We just met the man," Steph yelped. "Give him a minute! We shouldn't grill him!"

"I wasn't grilling! I was simply pointing out that art speaks. He listened. Now he's at a table with the artist, so he should let us listen!"

"Just..." Steph said.

I interrupted.

"Steph, it's okay. Thanks for protecting me. It's honestly incredibly comforting to have someone care. Really," I said, gesturing with my drink. "But, I think Grace is right. Why would I be here if it wasn't for her work? It's becoming increasingly obvious that I was meant to be here. And before you ask, I have no idea what that means either. But as I've moved East it seems like things have been placed in my path to help me along. Like right now, talking to you two, this isn't a normal thing for me to do. But I needed something like this. You know?"

I took a deep breath. My hands trembled.

"I loved a woman named ███. She and I were perfect. And not some bullshit Hollywood perfect, actual perfect... real world perfect. We shared odd ideas and thought them normal. I had a perfect love named ███. Three months ago she was killed in a car wreck..."

I paused and let my hands shake the two ice cubes in my drink. Grace and Steph both placed hands on my forearm.

They said nothing.

I stared at the amoeba table as it moved in a wet shimmer.

"She died. I had no idea what to do. I have no idea what to do. She was everything to me. She was the culmination of synchronicities, coincidences, fate, work, luck, karma and every prayer and meditation I've ever done. She died and with her died everything I ever remotely believed in. I died too. Every belief, faith, meaning I held... they all ended that day. They all burned. It all burned. Everything tasted like ash. I didn't know what to do. The walls were closing in. ████ was dead and I lost everything that made me a person."

I watched the table waver as I sipped from my drink, salty from tears.

"I'm sorry. I'm acting like an asshole. I should go. You didn't ask for this. This is stupid. It was nice meeting you," I spat out hurriedly.

I stood to run out. I was stopped by two vice-like grips on my forearm.

"No," they said in unison.

"There is no way we're letting you leave like this," Steph said. "Sit down, have a drink. You don't have to tell us about anything important. We can talk about art, or sports, or music, or whatever else. Come, sit. You're safe with us."

"Stay," said Grace simply.

I sat back down and wiped my eyes.

"Okay. Sorry. I'm a fucking mess."

"You're allowed to be a mess, Thomas," Steph said. "This is normal. You lost someone incredibly important to you. If you weren't 'a fucking mess' I'd be much more concerned."

We sat in silence. I sipped from my drink. They sipped from theirs. I excused myself to use the bathroom and get a fresh, non-tear-soaked drink. By the time I returned to the amoeba table I felt a little more human.

"Hi!" Grace and Steph said in a forcefully cheerful unison.

"Upbeat around here, huh?" I asked.

"We couldn't figure out how to make this less awkward. So we decided to make it more so!" Grace said.

"Appreciate it. Look... Christ," I pushed back the mess that was my hair and exhaled. "Here's why I'm here. When she was alive we made lists, one each. They were made up of lost and forgotten things from our pasts. It came from this weird book we both liked. We made our lists and promised to visit the place from the book. Well, after she was gone I couldn't think of any good reason for me to continue on. So, instead of killing myself, I quit my job and my life, and started driving East towards this crazy place that's supposed to house all the forgotten things. I know it's probably not real. But it's all I could think of doing. So, I've been driving East for a while now. I'm afraid to go where I think it could be, since, well, it's fictional. But where the fuck else should I go? So, I'm directionless, with only our lists as hope that I can find the impossible and maybe make this feel a little better. I just want to feel terrible... terrible would be a joy. I'm utterly shattered. I just want the slope to move upwards. So that's who I am. I'm a broken pile of shit that was once an incredibly lucky man, moving away from a void towards nothing. And, yeah, that's who you invited to ruin your evening."

My chin hit my chest as I stared into the table. I had laid it out for them. It was the truth. It was the first time that I felt the truth of it. I was a shattered person on a quest to kill windmills. The table gave no response.

"Go ahead if you want," Steph said as she grasped Grace's hand.

Grace looked down at the table too. As she began to speak she looked up into my eyes. Her giant blue eyes were wet with tears, her face set in grim determination.

"Six years ago I went to a party with my girlfriend. It wasn't a great relationship, but it was something. Well, she and I got into a fight. We were both pretty drunk and tended towards drama. I yelled. She yelled. The party watched. It was stupid, we were stupid kids. Well, she told me to find my own way home and she bailed. I was stuck at this party by myself. The night went on, and I started to feel weird. It was only me and like ten guys I didn't know..."

"Oh no," I interrupted without thinking.

"No, not that. Christ, I almost wish that was it. And yes, I know how terrible that sounds. They were really nice guys, it turns out. Well, a couple hours after she left there was a knock at the door. The policeman told us that my girlfriend was still alive, but in critical condition at the local hospital. She had run her car into a minivan outside the 7-Eleven down the road. A mother and two of her three children died at the scene..."

Steph held her.

I was stopped.

My throat hurt from holding back sobs.

We sat for minutes.

"I saw her at the hospital later," she said with a quavering voice. "I told the nurse I was her sister. Her actual sister and her mom were in the room. She had tubes come out of everywhere. I could barely see her face. Her mother gave me one look before throwing me out... I found out she was gone when her sister walked passed the waiting room screaming in tears. No one bothered to actually tell me that my girlfriend was dead. We had one stupid fight and four people were dead. Four fucking people. It takes a long time to feel like yourself after something like that- A long fucking time."

We sat in dead silence. An unseen jukebox started playing "Pale Blue Eyes" by the Velvet Underground. I felt that nothing more needed to be said of her story. She was open. We listened. I waited until Steph was done whispering into Grace's ear before I spoke.

"What would you put on your list, Steph?" I asked in the softest voice I could manage.

"My list? I don't know really. What am I allowed to put on it?" she asked.

"Anything. The place of lost and forgotten things has anything and everything you'd ever bother to think of."

"Oh... well..." she paused for a minute. "I think I'd want back my first Nintendo. I know I can get one now, but that first one meant so much. And maybe this frog I liked when I was little. That would be my list." Steph said.

"It's a good list." I tried to smile.

I took my collection of lists from my wallet and read aloud ██████'s and my own. They looked like they understood.

"What about you, Grace?" I asked.

"Nothing. Nothing at all. Nothing is ever truly lost, in the end. If I listed anything, it would make me feel like I was deficient. I'm not lacking for anything. I had my world taken from me, and I lived. There's nothing in me that makes me want that world back. I met

Steph as the person I am now. I learned from my losses and my pains to create that person. I hold onto what is lost inside of who I am now."

We sat in silence for moment before she continued.

"Anyway, if I ever made a list it would be a painting. And I wouldn't want it back. I'd want to memorialize the painting, the list, and move on with my life... and that's what I've done. So, mark my list with a #1 followed by some empty space. Maybe add my website at the bottom if they're really interested."

"Good list," I said.

"Yup, I'm a planner. Oh, speaking of which, get the fuck out of my town tomorrow."

"What? Why?"

"Because you have a stupid, honorable, wonderful goal that you have to meet, and I won't allow you to wait any longer to make it. Get out. Tomorrow morning you're gone. Drive to wherever it is you need to go. Light whatever candle you need to light, chant whatever it is you need to chant and move on with your life. You've done due diligence to your grief."

She touched my cheek with her hand, still wet and cold from holding her drink. Her eyes pierced me.

"Grace is right you know. Go east young man and find your lost things. The only thing keeping you away is your own fear. We get it, you don't know what to do besides feel horrible. You'll still feel horrible after you're done, but hopefully it'll be a new, manageable horrible. You'll find out how to be you again."

"I guess." I said.

"Nope. No guessing about it. You leave tomorrow morning. You drive to Lost-Ville, or wherever the fuck you're going, and you get better. We like you. We want you whole. Now agree with us immediately: you will leave tomorrow?"

I couldn't help but smile. Her demands were utterly charming. I downed my Scotch in one gulp.

"I'll go tomorrow and finish this." Once I heard my voice I knew it was true. I would press on to the place of lost things tomorrow.

"Good! Now, let us get fresh drinks and make complete drunken asses of ourselves!" Grace screamed.

She smiled. Her eyes radiated.

Steph beamed at her. She glowed.

I pictured walking into the place of forgotten things.

We drank and sang for hours. I felt almost human. I was happy I met them.

In the morning, I left without saying goodbye and walked bleary-eyed back to my motel. Eventually I found my car and pointed it East. It would take seventeen hours to get to the town from the book. It would take seventeen hours to end my journey.

6. The town

St. Paul was a sleep-deprived memory as I passed into New York state. I took a nap in the parking lot of an abandoned feed store when I realized how close I was. I was nearing the town where I thought the place of lost things existed.

Years ago, when ███ and I had talked about finding the place of lost things, I discovered a reference in another of the author's short stories to his hometown. It matched some of the details from his story about the place of lost things. The two places must be the same.

All these years later I was nearly there.

My heart sent quick anxiety shocks at random. I had left the highway an hour ago. My car's engine sounded like it was about to give up. The hill I was driving up was steep; my tank was nearly empty; my car crawled the last quarter mile to the top of the hill, sputtering. The top off the hill spit me out onto a small main street full of quaint "shoppes" replete with extraneous e's and p's. The place was old and wanted to make a few tourist bucks off its antiquity. The 7-Eleven-style gas station stuck out terribly. It looked as if it were deliberately designed to ruin the aesthetic. I hated myself for giving them my money, but my car's tank was empty and my bladder full.

I parked my car, brimming with fresh gasoline, in front of a very old parking meter. I fed it change until it stopped adding time. There's nothing I hate more than figuring out how long I'm meant to be somewhere. "Put in the maximum and let fate sort it out," is what I say. I've received many parking tickets because of this philosophy.

The main street wasn't particularly busy. The few cars that passed had that certain indefinable look of being local. The sidewalks were a few people short of bustling. It was nice. I spotted a small sign saying "Coffee" and walked towards it.

The coffee shop looked like a set from a 1940s movie. Its blue Formica table tops gleamed in the morning sun filtering through the lead glass windows. A milkshake bar ran across the rear, complete with dull-blue fake-leather seats. I took a seat at the bar. I could see through the little window into the kitchen. An elderly man nodded at me from his perch in front of a griddle. I nodded back.

"Hey, Bill! You got a customer!" he screamed.

I looked around for Bill. A customer in a rear booth looked around as well. Bill seemed to be a bit of a local mystery. A giant of a man lumbered out of an unseen back room. He was well over six feet tall and looked every part of 400lbs. He had a face which looked like it had taken more than its fair share of punches. He walked behind the bar to where I was sitting.

"Hi there," he rumbled at me. "What can I get ya?"

His voice was a resonant bass, with a slight hint of mischievous joy at the edges. His eyes were gleaming swimming pools of blue. He was one of those people you liked from word one.

"I could murder a cup of coffee."

"You got it. One victim coming right up."

After sliding a laminated menu in my direction, he walked to the coffee station. A moment later a gently placed cup was in front of me. I asked what was good. He asked where I was from. I told him. He answered at length. I ordered something called a Taylor Ham, egg, and cheese sandwich. It was brilliant. Taylor ham tasted like the result of the copulation of a pig and a salt lick.

The giant stood near the window chatting with the cook as I finished up. He refilled my coffee without asking. I loved this man.

"Pardon, but have you ever heard of something in this area called something like 'the place of lost things' or the like?" I asked.

"Yup, I sure have. It's not really that big of a town," he smiled warmly.

That was not the answer I expected. I had thought it would be harder to find... a hidden secret only known to special initiates.

"What's the deal with it?"

"How do ya mean?"

"Well, it's in this book and…"

"I know the book. He was a local kid… used to sit in the corner booth, writing and smoking cigarettes all night."

"Oh! You know him?"

"I can't say that I knew him, but we shared words over the years. Nice enough guy, but a little on the weirdo side, you know?"

"Weirdo side?" I asked.

"He was one of those kids that loved to look sad, even when I knew he was in a good mood. Personally, I think it's weird to try to be sad. Most of us got plenty of reasons for that without making up more. But, don't get me wrong, he was a good guy. Wouldn't hurt a fly, very polite."

"I get that. So, did he run the lost things place or something?"

"Nope, some other fella runs it. He doesn't come down too often, lives in the hills."

"So, it's real? It's an actual, brick and mortar building?"

"Not sure what it's made of, to be honest," he smiled at his jest. "But, yes, it's up there and real as this place."

I paused to collect myself, taking a pull from the still warm coffee.

"Huh… I didn't realize until this moment that I wasn't expecting it to be there."

"Makes sense, in that the place doesn't make any sense so why would it be there?"

"Jesus, I guess I really am going to go there. Where is it from here?"

He gave me directions. They were rudimentary, lacking road names. Strangely, those were the exact kind that I was good at following.

"Thank you sir, really appreciate it. You think they're open?"

"Far as I know they are. I don't make it a habit of heading up that way. You lose something?"

"Something like that. I think. I dunno. At this point I think I'm just finishing up an idea because it seemed like the right thing to do."

"Good. I like when you guys get a good ending."

"Us guys?"

"You're hardly the first person to wander through here looking for the place of lost stuff. We get a few every year. Most of them looked far worse for wear than you. You're the type to find something good up there. I'm excited for you."

"Thanks, that's really nice to hear."

"Yup. Well, you get going young man. If you need some food on the way back, you know where to find us."

He shook my hand and picked up the stack of bills I'd left next to my coffee cup. A bell I didn't hear on the way in jingled as I closed the door behind me. There was nothing left to do but finish what we started all these years ago, when there was still something to call a 'we.'

7. *On the way to the place of lost things*

The instructions from the giant in the coffee shop lead me through a labyrinthine sequence of streets into a wooded, hilly area above the town. Walking was supposed to be much easier than driving, and the coffee shop giant had said there would be obvious short cuts. The streets began to curve in on themselves nearly completing a circle before they shot back out at violent angles. It looked like the medical chart of a heart attack, or the waveform of random noises hiding behind orchestras. I walked in near circles until a jutting turn would spit me further up the hill. I had no idea how these streets could ever have evolved organically. It was as if they were made to be unnavigable – a line from the book echoed in my head. This was the area the shop existed in. it was supposed to be confusing. It was supposed to be unique. After yet another jagged turn, I felt heartened and pressed forward into the unknown.

Turning yet another severe right, I walked through a stand of trees. Before me sat a dilapidated set of buildings. The leftmost was covered in peeling, dirty, white paint. The windows were cracked, but intact. Above the door was a faded sign reading "The House of Newly Formed Isotopes." The building on the right was covered in grayish, moldy, shingles. The structure looked crooked, slightly leaning left. Above the listing door frame hung a sign reading: "Broken and Forgotten Things Inside."

I had found it.

I was too nervous to go in right away, so I paced the area. My pacing did not help, so I decided to see what was in The House of Newly Formed Isotopes. It was not what I was expecting. Opening the front door revealed a lushly appointed room full of leather chairs and low tables. A bar ran the leftmost wall, behind which hundreds of bottles stood in various states of fullness. The bottles were lit from below with dozens of different colored lights, making the shelves appear almost alchemical. I started to see where the name came from. This must have been where the writer of the book went. I was still too excited to go next door. I was afraid of what was to come, so I snaked through the comfortable looking leather chairs and sat down on a barstool. The counter was made of pressed copper, dented, with spots of darkened patina. It was incredibly comfortable. I waited for the bartender while reading the oddly lit labels. I waited a couple minutes then began to grow uncomfortable. I searched the bar for a bell to ring, or sign to read. Nothing presented itself. I coughed lightly. I waited. I coughed slightly louder. I waited more, all the while feeling anxious because I hated people who coughed for attention.

"Hi!" I said somewhat louder than a conversational level. "You open? Anyone around?"

I listened for a response, feeling stupid. Why was I sitting at a bar inside a fictional building? Why was I on the east coast? The senselessness of my trip started to weigh on me. What was I expecting here? Was this simply running away from ███'s memory? Was this honoring her as I first intended? I felt silly. I felt lost. I, after five minutes in an empty bar, finally felt like having a drink. It was auspicious timing.

A man in his mid-40s emerged from a door on the far end of the bar. He smiled to me and nodded. He washed his hands, tied on an apron, and moved to stand in front of me.

"What can I get you?" He said in a soporific baritone.

"Oh, Jesus, I didn't even think about it. Sorry." I apologized.

"We get that a lot. Want something from the local drink list?"

"What's that?"

"A list of drinks we invented – 'we' being myself and the place next door."

The bartender gestured with his head.

"Oh, yes. Yeah, that would be good."

"Green okay?"

"Yes?" I said, cautiously.

"Don't worry, you look like the green type. I have a sense for this sorta thing."

He turned his back to me and grabbed a few bottles from the area underlit with green light. I couldn't see the labels as he mixed liquids together and shook the mix in a steel cup. He poured the mix into a tumbler and placed it before me.

It was far from green. It looked, and smelled, like whiskey.

"Thanks," I offered him my card. "Keep it open?"

He nodded his assent.

The drink tasted like clouds. It was perfect. It danced on my tongue and took a joyous water slide down my throat.

"Holy fuck!" I cried. "What is this?"

"You like it?" He asked in his calm, measured voice.

"Like it? It's amazing. It's really... holy shit, wow. Can I have another of the same, please?"

"No." He said.

"What?"

"Doesn't work like that."

"What doesn't?"

"This place. It's for new isotopes. You can't go back to the same thing. Figured if you made it this far you'd know that."

"Well... I guess... shit... I guess I never figured that part out. I was so focused on the place of lost things."

"I understand. We get your type in here pretty often. The joint next door is for all that repeat business, do-it-the-same style of stuff. It's a good business model. I don't cotton to all that. I like the past where it is. Want another?"

"Oh, well, okay. One more of not the same."

The bartender smiled.

"There you go. I'll get you something purple. You get a nice purple in you and then you pop in next door."

He pulled a single bottle from the purple lighted shelf and poured it over ice into two tumblers.

"Here you go," he handed me a shot glass. "To our health."

He raised his glass and finished it in one; I did the same. It was whiskey.

"That was whiskey."

"Yeah, well, everything can't be magical. I figure you're going next door, might as well load up on a little liquid courage."

"I think you're right. How about one more purple and settle up?"

I scribbled my name on some paper, threw back a shot of something that tasted like sophomore year in high school, and left while waving over my shoulder.

The light outside burned my eyes.

I felt tipsy.

I floated over the few steps to the place next door.

I took a deep breath and placed my shaking hand on the handle.

I opened the door to the place of forgotten things.

8. In the place of forgotten things

The light was the color of memories: a dust-drenched sepia mimicking all pasts simultaneously. This was the place from the book, from my imagination. It was exactly what it needed to be: a brown drink from a green shelf. It was exactly what was needed for exactly who needed it.

The room was full. Every available space was covered in trinkets, books, tiny skeletons, coins, bits of paper – all of which sat under layers of dust. In between the tables covered in dust and ephemera were a series of card catalog cabinets. I barely remembered card catalogs from my earliest schooling. They were incomprehensible boxes which dominated the center of my elementary school library. They were the domain of teachers, older kids, and the elusive creatures called 'librarians'. I remembered card catalogs. This room was made from card catalogs. They stretched from front to back, side to side, in seemingly endless rows. The room was a hive of card-filled cabinets, and curio covered tables – save for a desk on the right-most side.

The desk was covered in unstacked papers and random cards. On the corner of the desk sat a bell. I walked through the cabinets towards the bell. I rang. I waited. I rang. I waited. I waited. I rang. I wandered.

I walked through the maze of card cabinets, opening a drawer or two in each. They were all full of lists. Drawers and drawers of lists, all in different hand writing, all on different paper, but lists all the same. I'd pull a card out at random; it would read something like:

1) My action man Tony stole before he moved
2) The picture of me and Ericka at the prom
3) My mother

Or,

1) A sense of worth

2) The ability to be alone

3) Thoughts of life that weren't terrible

Or.

1) Mellissa

2) Mellissa

3) Mellissa

4) Mellissa

Or.

1) Who I was when I was with Michael

2) Who I was when I was with Michael

3) Who I was when I was with Michael

4) Who I was when I was with Michael

5) Who I was when I was with Michael

6) Who I was when I was with Michael

Or.

1) The feeling of reading it the first time

2) The love I felt then

3) His reaction

Some of them would be empty, stained with tears.

Others would be a picture of a child, a wife, a husband, a dog,

a car.

Some would be a folded napkin with a liquid stained phone

number written on it.

Some were objects: A dead cellphone with a puncture on the bottom to slide with the cards; a trinket from a vending machine; a lock of hair; a Pez dispenser; a scrap of cloth.

The cabinets stretched on and on. I rang the bell again. I waited. I rang the bell again. I waited. I looked at the desk and noticed a small scrap of paper sticking out from under a magazine for movie enthusiasts. I pulled it out. The writing looked familiar. Maybe – Could it be?

It read:

I am so glad you made it here. I will love you forever.
Please please please place our lists in the cabinet nearest the window.
Think of me sometimes. I'll be under that window if you need.

Goodbye, my love.

It was unsigned.

It was so familiar.

She was never here. How could it be hers?

She was never here.

But she would have liked the area nearest the window. That was correct.

Could it be hers?

I followed the instructions.

It must be hers.

I placed the list in the topmost shelf nearest the window. I placed my list behind it.

The sepia light swallowed the cards as they settled into their spots. A line of shadow enveloped the lists as I closed the drawer.

It shut with a dull thud.

I walked out of the room of forgotten things without looking back.

Once outside, I took a breath and began to walk down a spiraling path to a town in which I didn't belong

For the first time since I left Portland, I found myself without a destination, without a list, without the suffocation of her loss.

Our lists were archived in the place of lost things, and I was once again alive. I was alive, and no longer guilt-ridden for it. I was alive.

ABOUT THE AUTHOR

Alexx's previous works include the novel *Periphery* and a poetry/short prose collection *the void sutras.*

Outside of writing, he hosts the long running *Alexxcast,* as well as the film review podcast *John and Alexx Hate Stuff.*

More information can be found at:

Alexxcast.com

Johnandalexxatestuff.com

alexxbollen.com

www.ingramcontent.com/pod-product-compliance
Lightning Source LLC
Chambersburg PA
CBHW070342120726
47909CB00008B/2722